Little Black Dress

JAMES PATTERSON

WITH EMILY RAYMOND

BOOK**SHOTS**

1 3 5 7 9 10 8 6 4 2

BookShots
20 Vauxhall Bridge Road
London SW1V 2SA

BookShots is part of the Penguin Random House group of companies
whose addresses can be found at global.penguinrandomhouse.com

 Penguin
Random House
UK

First published by BookShots in 2016

www.penguin.co.uk

A CIP catalogue record for this book is available from the British Library.

ISBN 9781786530073

Printed and bound in Great Britain by Clays Ltd, St Ives Plc

 MIX
Paper from
responsible sources
FSC® C018179

Penguin Random House is committed to a sustainable future
for our business, our readers and our planet. This book is made
from Forest Stewardship Council® certified paper.

Little
Black
Dress

PROLOGUE

I SPOTTED IT ON the Bergdorf sale rack: see-through black chiffon layered over a simple black sheath, cut to skim lightly over the hips and fall just above the knee. Paired with a thin gold belt, there was something Grecian, even goddessy, about it.

It was somehow subtle yet spectacular. Not a dress, but a *Dress*.

When I tried it on, I was no longer Jane Avery, age thirty-five, overworked editor at Manhattan's *Metropolitan* magazine and recent divorcée. I was Jane Avery, age none of your business, a card-carrying member of the media elite, a woman who was single and proud of it.

Even at 40 percent off, the Dress was a minor fortune. I decided to buy it anyway.

And that purchase changed everything.

CHAPTER 1

IN THE OPULENT LIMESTONE lobby of the Four Seasons New York, I handed over my Amex. "A city-view king, please." No tremor in my voice at all. Nothing to betray the pounding of my heart, the adrenaline flooding my veins.

Am I really about to do this?

Maybe I should have had another glass of rosé.

The desk clerk tapped quickly on her keyboard. "We have a room on the fortieth floor," she said. "Where are you two visiting from?"

I shot a glance over my shoulder. *Honestly? About twenty-five blocks from here.* My knees were turning into Jell-O.

Behind me, Michael Bishop, a thumb hooked in the belt loop of his jeans, flashed his gorgeous smile—first at me, then at the clerk. "Ohio, miss," he said, giving his muscled shoulders an aw-shucks shrug. His eyes were green as jade. "Mighty big city you got here, darlin'," he said, a drawl slipping into his voice.

"Oh—Ohio," the clerk repeated, like it was the most beautiful word she'd ever heard. She looked like she was unbuttoning his shirt with her eyes as she handed me the room key.

Very unprofessional, if you ask me.

But then again, how professional was it to check into a hotel with one of *Metropolitan*'s freelance writers—who, by the way, had obviously never even *been* to Ohio?

If he had, he'd have known they don't talk like cowboys there.

Michael Bishop lived on the Lower East Side of Manhattan; I lived on the Upper West Side. We'd known each other since our first years in the magazine business. Today we'd met for lunch, to go over a story he was writing for *Metropolitan*. The café, an elegant little French place with fantastic *jambon beurre* sandwiches, was close to my office.

It was also close to the Four Seasons.

We'd laughed, we'd had a glass of rosé—and now, suddenly, we were here.

Am I really about to do this?

"If you want tickets to a Broadway show or reservations at Rao's, the concierge can assist you," the clerk offered. By now she'd taken off Michael's shirt and was licking his chest.

"Actually," I said, "we have other plans." I grabbed Michael's hand and pulled him into the elevator before I lost my nerve.

We stood in front of our reflections in the gold-mirrored doors. "Really?" I said to mirror-Michael, who was as gorgeous as the real Michael but yellower. *"Ohio?"*

He laughed. "I know, Jane—you're a former fact-checker, so the truth is very important to you," he said. "I, however, am a writer, and I take occasional *liberties* with it." He stepped closer to me, and then he slipped an arm around my waist. "Nice dress, by the way," he said.

"Do you also take occasional liberties with your editors?" I asked, trying to be playful.

He shook his head. "Never," he said.

I believed him—but it didn't matter either way. This had been *my* idea.

It wasn't about loneliness, or even simple lust (though that obviously played a part). I just wanted to know if I could do something like this without feeling weird or cheap.

I still wasn't sure.

The hotel room was a gleaming, cream-colored box of understated luxury. A bottle of Chardonnay waited in a silver wine bucket, and there were gourmet chocolates arranged on the pillows. Through the giant windows, Manhattan glittered, a spectacle of steel and glass.

I stood in the center of the beautiful room, holding my purse against my body like a kind of shield. I was charged and excited and   all of a sudden   a little bit scared.

This was new territory for me. If I didn't turn tail and run right now, I was about to do something I'd barely even had the guts to imagine.

Michael, his green eyes both gentle and hungry, took the purse from my hands and placed it on a chair. Straightening up again, he brushed my hair away from my neck, and then he kissed me, gently, right above my collarbone. A shiver ran down my spine.

"Is this okay?" he asked softly.

I remembered the way he'd kissed my fingers at the café. I remembered how I'd said to him, *Let's get out of here.*

I wanted this.

"Yes," I breathed. "It's more than okay."

His lips moved up my neck, his tongue touching my skin ever so lightly. He traced a finger along my jawline and then slowly drew it down again, stopping at the low neckline of the Dress.

I waited, trembling, for him to slip his hand inside the silk.

But he didn't. He paused, barely breathing. And then he reached around my back and found the slender zipper between my shoulder blades. He gave it a sharp tug, and the black silk slid down my body in a whisper. I stood there—exposed, breathless, thrilled—and then Michael crushed his lips to mine.

We kissed deeply. Hungrily. I ran my palms up his strong arms, his broad shoulders. He reached under me and lifted me up, and I wrapped my legs around his waist. He tasted like wine.

I whispered my command: *"Take me to bed."* Then I added, "Please."

"So polite," he murmured into my hair. "Anything you say, Jane."

He carried me to the giant bed and laid me down on it. His fingers found my nipples through the lace of my bra, and then my bra, too, seemed to slip off my body, and his mouth was where his fingers had been.

I gasped.

Yes, oh yes. I'm really doing this.

His tongue teased me, pulled at me. His hands seemed to be everywhere at once. "Should I—" he began.

I said, "Don't talk, just do." I did not add *Please* this time.

I wriggled out of my panties as he undressed, and then he was naked before me, golden in the noon light, looking like some kind of Greek demigod descended from Mount Olympus.

I stretched up my arms and Michael fell into them. He kissed me again as I arched to meet him. When he thrust himself inside me, I cried out, rocking against his hips, kissing his shoulder, his neck, his chin. I pulled him into me with all my strength as the heat inside me rose in waves. When I cried out in release, my nails dug into Michael's shoulders. A moment later he cried out too, and then he collapsed on top of me, panting.

I couldn't believe it. I'd really done it.

Spent, we both slept for a little while. When I awoke, Michael was standing at the end of the bed, his shirt half buttoned, his golden chest still visible. A smile broke over his gorgeous face.

"Jane Avery, that was an incredible lunch," Michael Bishop said. "Could I interest you in dinner?"

I smiled back at him from the tangle of ivory sheets. As perfect as he was, as *this* had been, today was a one-time deal. I wasn't ready to get involved again. "Actually," I said, "thank you, but I have other plans."

He looked surprised. A guy like Michael wasn't used to being turned down. "Okay," he said after a moment. "I get it."

I doubted that he did.

It's not you, I thought, *it's me.*

After he kissed me good-bye—sweetly, longingly—I turned on the water in the deep porcelain tub. I'd paid seven hundred dollars for this room and I might as well enjoy it a little longer.

I sank into the bath, luxuriant with lavender-scented bubbles. It was crazy, what I'd done. But I'd loved it.

And I didn't feel cheap. *Au contraire:* I felt *rich*.

CHAPTER 2

I SWIPED A FREE Perrier from the office fridge—one of the perks of working at *Metropolitan*—and hurried to my desk, only to find Brianne, my best friend and the magazine's ad sales director, draped dramatically across its cluttered surface.

"You took the looooongest lunch," she said accusingly. "We were supposed to get cappuccinos at Ground Central."

"I'm sorry," I said distractedly. I could see the message light on my phone blinking. "My meeting…um, my meeting didn't exactly go as planned. I'm going to have to work late tonight."

"Oh, *merde*." She gave a long, theatrical sigh. *"Pas encore."*

I couldn't help smiling. Brianne was one-quarter French; the rest of her was full-blown New Jersey. On a good day, she was funny and loud, as effervescent as a glass of Champagne; on a bad day she was like Napoleon with lipstick and PMS.

"Can we do it tomorrow?" I asked.

Bri still looked sulky. "You realize, don't you, that you stay late because you're avoiding your complete lack of a social life?"

"I stay because I care about my job." I tugged discreetly at my bra. Somehow I'd managed to put it on wrong.

"So do I," Bri said, "but you don't see me here at nine p.m. on a Friday."

"You're in a different department," I said, unwilling to admit that she had a point.

She took one of my blue editing pencils and twisted her pretty auburn hair around it, making an artfully messy bun. "I was going to set you up on a date tonight, you know."

"We've gone over this, Bri," I said firmly. "I'm not interested."

Bri lifted herself from my desk and stood before me with her hands on her hips. Five inches shorter than me, she had to crane her neck up. "I know how much you love your Netflix-and-Oreo nights, honey. But it's time you got back into the game."

I *did* love those nights, even though I'd be the first to admit that too many of them in a row got depressing. "I'm not ready to date, Bri. I like the sidelines."

Bri held up a manicured finger. "First of all, you've been divorced for almost a year and a half."

"Thanks for keeping track," I said.

Bri held up another finger. "Second of all, this guy's practically perfect."

"Then you date him," I suggested. "You're single now too. Aren't you? Or did you fall in love again last night?"

Bri giggled. She gave her heart away like it was candy on

Halloween. "There's the *cutest* guy in my spinning class," she admitted. She drifted off into a dreamy reverie for a moment. Then she shook her head and snapped back to attention. "Hey. You're changing the subject. We're talking about you and your nonexistent sex life."

A blush flared hot on my cheeks.

Bri immediately widened her eyes at me. Her mouth fell open, and then she nearly shouted, "Oh my God. You got laid last night!"

I looked wildly around. "Shhh!" I hissed. My boss's assistant was five feet away at the Xerox machine. She didn't seem to have heard Bri's accusation, though. Turning back to my friend, I made an effort to keep a straight face. To look serious and professional. "I did *not* get laid last night," I said.

I got laid an hour ago.

Bri's merry brown eyes grew narrow. "The more I look at you, the more I think there's something different about you today," she said.

I shrugged. "Well, I'm wearing a new dress." I gave a little twirl. "Isn't it fantastic?"

Bri's skeptical expression softened—but barely. "If you weren't the most honest person I've ever met, I'd swear you were lying to me, Jane Avery."

I smiled. "I'd never lie to you, hon," I said.

But I might stretch the truth.

"Are you sure you won't go out tonight?" she wheedled. "I want you to find a good man."

I sucked in my breath. My mood suddenly shifted. "I thought I had," I said.

Bri looked at me sympathetically. "I'm sorry you married a bastard, Janie. He fooled us all," she said. "But one error shouldn't ban you from the playing field."

I rubbed the spot where the big diamond ring used to be. James had loved me, he really had—but he'd also loved his ex-girlfriend. And her sister.

"Enough with the sports metaphors, Bri," I pleaded.

Bri mimed a baseball swing. "You gotta step up to the plate," she said, smirking, just to annoy me.

"And *you've* gotta get back to your own desk," I said, laughing. "I have work to do."

Bri walked reluctantly to the door and then turned back around. "Don't you want to know who your date was going to be?"

"Not really." I picked up my phone and pressed the messages button.

"Michael Bishop," she said as she walked away. "He is soooo handsome."

The receiver fell to my desk with a clunk.

Step up to the plate, Bri? I thought. *I did—and Michael Bishop was my home run.*

CHAPTER 3

WALKING INTO AL'S DINER at 90th and Columbus after work that evening, I inhaled the familiar smell of grease and burned coffee—and underneath that, the subtle whiff of good olive oil, salty feta, and ripe heirloom tomatoes. My mouth watered as I slid into my familiar booth. Al's Diner looked like just another greasy spoon, but I knew its secret: *kolokitho keftedes* and *dolmades*—aka zucchini fritters and stuffed grape leaves—so delicious you'd swear you were on Santorini.

Al Dimitriou spotted me and lumbered out of the kitchen, wiping his hands on his stained apron. "Janie, *koreetsi mou*," he said. *My girl.* "It's late! Either you already ate and you're here for baklava…or you worked too long and you're starving."

"Door number two," I said, smiling at him.

Al shook his head at me. "You work too hard, Jane-*itsa*," he said. He turned and hollered, "Veta, Janie's here!"

"I know, I know!" Veta, Al's wife, came hurrying over with a basket of pita and a bowl of baba ghanoush. It took all my self-control to say *hello* and *thank you* before I started shoveling it into my mouth. Veta patted my head and gave me a quick maternal once-over. "You look very pretty tonight, Janie," she said. "Although the table manners..." She nudged me affectionately.

"Sorry," I mumbled. "Famished."

Al looked at me more carefully. "You got a date after this?"

Why does everyone in New York City care about my dating life?

"No such plans," I said, my mouth still full of warm pita and smoky eggplant.

Veta, who was as quick and petite as Al was big and slow, swatted him on his giant shoulder. "Just because she looks extra beautiful tonight doesn't mean she's going to see a man," she scolded. "Don't be so old-fashioned."

Al shrugged good-naturedly. "I was just making conversation."

"Just sticking your nose in a lady's business," Veta countered. She turned to me. "Don't mind the big lug," she said.

"I don't mind him," I said. "I love him."

At that, Al got slightly red and excused himself, saying something about needing to check on some fava beans.

Veta sat down across from me. She grinned. "So—do you?"

"Do I what?" I asked. I was having a hard time concentrating on anything other than the rich, delicious *meze*. I found an olive and popped it into my mouth.

"Have a date, you goose."

"No, Veta!" I exclaimed. "Why on earth—"

She ducked her head in embarrassment. "Sorry, sorry," she said. "I guess I was hoping."

"You don't need to hope for me," I said. "I'm happy."

And I was *very* happy right now. My God, the baba ghanoush…

Veta gazed thoughtfully out the window, where a flock of pigeons feasted on a discarded loaf of Wonder Bread. Then she turned back to me and said, "So, my happy Janie, do you want the lamb or the octopus?"

I laughed at her matter-of-factness. "Chef's choice," I said.

She patted my hand. "We'll take good care of you," she said.

"You always do," I said, because it was true.

It might have looked like I was sitting alone in a diner on a Friday night, but as far as I was concerned, I was having dinner with friends.

CHAPTER 4

BY THE TIME I said good-bye to Al and Veta, night had fallen. Metal grates covered the doors of the Laundromat, the shoe boutique, and the store that specialized in four-hundred-dollar throw pillows. But cars and cabs still swept by on Columbus Avenue. Couples on dates strolled along, the women tottering in high, uncomfortable heels.

One of the benefits of being 5'8": you can just say no to stilettos.

As I stood on the corner, waiting to cross, I could see the light in my third-floor kitchen, burning small and yellow and alone.

Netflix and Oreos, here I come, I thought.

Just then, the wind caught the skirt of the Dress. The black silk seemed to swirl away from me, like there was a different direction it wanted to go in.

And why *should* I go home? I didn't have a dog or cat—I didn't even have a fish. The most I'd had was a cactus. (By the way, don't believe the hype about cacti: you *can* kill them, and it's not even hard.)

A little way down the block, the Teddy's Piano Bar sign blinked invitingly. The tiny watering hole had been there since the 1920s, when it was a speakeasy full of smoke and music, fueled by bathtub gin.

I'd never gone inside. But tonight, I walked straight toward it.

The walls were covered in abstract murals painted by some famous, long-dead artist. At the piano, a silver-haired man with a truly enormous nose played Gershwin. Couples chatted at small, cozy tables, and candlelight flickered on the murals, turning them into swirls of color and line.

I ordered a French 75 and sank into a banquette.

"Summertime, and the livin' is easy," sang a black-haired beauty who'd joined the old man on the bench.

I smiled; I'd always loved that song. But I couldn't carry a tune in a Kate Spade handbag, so I hummed along quietly.

At the table next to me, a man sat alone with an unopened book and a glass of amber liquid. He'd taken off his tie and tucked it into the breast pocket of his gray linen suit. His fingers tapped along to the music.

I noted the lack of a wedding ring.

He had a good profile—deep-set eyes and a strong chin. I watched him out of the corner of my eye.

Should I? I thought. *I definitely shouldn't.*

But then I changed my mind.

I waited until the song had ended, and then I slid from the

banquette into the chair next to him. "Is this seat taken?" I asked.

The man looked up, startled. His dark eyebrows lifted. He smiled at me—a slow, almost shy smile. "I guess it is now," he said.

"I'm Jane," I said. "Hi."

"Hello, Jane, I'm Aiden," he said. He nodded toward my glass. "I'd buy you a drink, but you seem to have one already."

I clinked my cocktail to his and took a sip of the bubbly liquid. "You can buy the next round."

He laughed. "What if I bore you before that?"

I gave him my best mock-frown. "Don't tell me you have self-esteem problems, Aiden," I said. "You don't look the type."

He shrugged. "Let's just say I wasn't expecting a beautiful woman to sit down at my table tonight," he said.

Please, I'm not beautiful—that's what I almost said. But then I glanced down at my perfect, elegant Dress and felt a surge of confidence. What if, in calling me beautiful, Aiden was actually *right?* I smiled, sipped delicately at my drink, and made a new rule for myself: *If life hands you a compliment, take it.*

"This is a nice place," I said, looking around the dim, inviting room. "Do you come here often?" Then I felt like kicking myself for delivering such a cliché of a line.

Aiden swirled his whiskey and the ice clicked in the glass. "You could call me a regular, I guess. The guy at the piano is my uncle."

I looked at the homely silver-haired player again. "Hard to see the family resemblance," I said skeptically.

Aiden said, "Really? I think we look exactly alike."

"Aha! You *do* have a self-esteem problem," I said.

He grinned. "You have an understanding-sarcasm problem," he countered.

I laughed. I felt slightly tipsy, but it wasn't from the drink—I'd barely touched it. It was from being out on a Friday night and flirting with a handsome stranger.

I'd already done *one* thing I never thought I'd do today. Why stop there?

"So what do you do, Jane?" Aiden asked.

I shook my head. "Let's not talk about work."

Aiden looked disappointed. "You mean I don't get the chance to tell you about my fascinating work in maritime law?"

I leaned closer. "Do you prosecute pirates—with peg legs and hooks for hands?"

"If only," he said ruefully.

"Then I'm not interested." I sat back and crossed my arms. "You'll have to come up with a better topic for discussion."

Aiden laughed. "And now the beautiful woman makes conversational demands," he said.

I giggled. But I didn't let myself apologize.

And so this handsome stranger told me the story of his former cycling career, including the time he crashed on the Giro d'Italia, Italy's version of the Tour de France, and finished the day's race with a face dripping blood.

I liked the way he moved closer to me to tell it, the way he kept his voice low so he wouldn't disrupt his uncle's playing.

The song was "Memory," from *Cats,* and half the bar was mouthing the words.

I was allergic to cats. And *Cats.*

But I liked the feeling of Aiden's breath near my ear.

"—and then the race was momentarily stopped by cows in the road!" he was saying. "And the guy next to me is yelling *'Porca vacca!'* Which means 'pig cow,' literally, but also means 'damn it'—"

His face shone with the memory. He looked so happy and alive that before I knew what I was doing, I'd put my hand on top of his.

He stopped talking immediately. His eyes met mine, dark and questioning.

The room at the Four Seasons was mine until tomorrow at 11 a.m.

I knew that Aiden would go wherever I asked him to. Do whatever I wanted him to do.

He'd tell me cycling stories all night. Or serenade me while his uncle played John Lennon's "Imagine." Or he'd slip the Dress from my shoulders and make love to me until I was cross-eyed.

Wait a second: was I absolutely *insane?*

"Jane," he said, his voice suddenly husky.

I gazed into his dark eyes. My heart was thumping wildly.

I made a decision.

I said softly, "It's been so nice to meet you. But I have to go."

And then I picked up my handbag and dashed out of the bar. As I ran down the street, the strains of "The Music of the Night" faded behind me until I could hear nothing but the wind.

CHAPTER 5

THE NEXT DAY, I decided to take a last-minute getaway. Outside the city, I could fill my lungs with clean air and my mind with clean thoughts.

My mistake was going to my sister's house in Westchester.

Mylissa was four years older than me, but ever since my divorce she'd been acting like my mother. Five minutes into my visit she told me I needed a haircut and highlights. An hour later, she tried to set me up with a divorced suburban lawyer who raced vintage cars in his spare time.

I knew she was trying to help, but it bothered me. Sure, Mylissa had a beautiful house, a loving husband, and a perfect pair of eight-year-old daughters, but none of this made her an expert on *my* life.

"You're not much of an expert on it either," she huffed.

Point taken.

We ended up having a nice weekend, eating and drinking and gossiping about her neighbors. But I had to admit I was glad to leave.

It was late Sunday evening by the time I got back to Manhattan. But instead of hurrying home to the peace, quiet, and potentially depressing solitude of my bedroom, I found myself walking into the Campbell Apartment, the upscale bar inside Grand Central Terminal.

I took a seat at the mahogany bar. As my eyes adjusted to the dim light, I wondered if I'd made a mistake in coming here. It was like Valentine's Day in June: everywhere I looked, someone was canoodling with someone else, sharing vintage cocktails, artisanal cheese plates, and deep, romantic glances.

"I'd recommend the Prohibition Punch and a bowl of truffled popcorn," said a voice, stiff with formality and a British accent.

I looked up to see a bow-tied, young bartender vigorously polishing a champagne flute.

"It's just too *sad* to eat an entire artisanal cheese plate alone, isn't it?" I asked wryly.

The bartender promptly lost his professional decorum by cracking up. "Absolutely not," he said, grinning. "You could eat anything you wanted and it wouldn't be sad." He leaned forward and whispered, "But between the two of us, the Ardrahan smells funkier than an Iowa pig farm and the Époisses has the bouquet of well-used gym towel."

Now it was my turn to laugh. He was cute *and* funny—like a blond Eddie Redmayne, accent and everything. "In that case, I'll have the popcorn," I said.

"Excellent choice, miss," he said, taking a step back and clearly trying to regain his gravitas.

I raised an eyebrow at him. "Please, don't get stuffy again. I tip better when I'm entertained."

"I shall dispense with the straight face," he said solemnly. "And I would be most honored to entertain you." And then he offered me a huge, goofy grin. "Wanna see my Arnold Schwarzenegger impression?"

I most certainly did. He looked quickly around—checking for his boss, no doubt—and then he cocked his head, hunched his shoulders, and transformed into the Terminator as he mixed my cocktail.

I clapped. "You must be an actor," I said.

"Me and every other bartender in town," he said.

"Tough way to make a living?" I asked sympathetically.

For a second he looked slightly chagrined. "Yeah. But just you wait," he said, brightening. "Someday you'll go to the movies and my face'll be up there, twenty feet tall, and you'll go, *I know that guy! He made me a great drink.*"

"And he forgot to put in the order for the popcorn," I added.

He flushed, embarrassed. "Wow, I'm not doing my job very well, am I?"

"Well, if part of your job is entertaining a single girl in a couples' bar, then you deserve a raise," I said.

"Single, huh?" he said, raising an eyebrow.

I shrugged, as if to say, *Maybe not for long.*

Because I had the sudden idea that he and I would make a great couple.

For about two hours.

You don't even know his name, Jane! said the small voice of my sanity.

So ask him, and then see when he gets off work, said a different voice entirely.

When he put the popcorn in front of me, we both took a big handful. But suddenly we were both too shy to speak.

Then I said, "I think—" at the same time that he said, "Do you want—"

We laughed awkwardly. It was like being in seventh grade again.

We were saved by a pearl-bedecked waitress, who appeared by my elbow with a cheese plate. "Kitchen made an extra," she said to my English bartender. "You guys want this?"

I grinned at him. "Eau de barnyard," I said. "And I don't even have to eat it alone."

"You never know when you're going to get lucky," he said. Then, obviously feeling more confident, he flashed me a rakish grin. "Right?"

The double entendre was extremely clear. I smiled back at him, imagining all the possibilities. For one thing, no one had talked dirty to me in an English accent before.

But the small voice of my sanity was trying to make itself heard. *Go home and go to bed,* it said. *Alone,* it clarified.

I picked up the parsley garnish and nervously ripped it into green confetti.

What am I going to do?

"Hey," he said, "Earth to—"

"Jane," I said. "And you are…?"

"Thom," he said. "With an *h*."

"Thom," I said quickly, "can I get your number?"

He looked confused. But he scribbled it onto a napkin and handed it to me. I tucked it into my purse. Then I laid down fifty dollars and blew him a kiss.

"I'll call you," I said.

Even though I knew I wouldn't.

You're a coward, Jane, I thought as I hurried down the steps to the train station.

No, you're very smart.

CHAPTER 6

I HAD A *METROPOLITAN* editorial meeting at 10 a.m. At eight, though, clutching a takeout coffee half the size of my torso, I strode into the office of my therapist, Alex Jensen, PhD, and blurted, "Do you think I'm crazy?"

Dr. Jensen looked up at me and smiled. He was fortyish, attractive in a bookish way; he squinted whenever he wasn't wearing his glasses, which was most of the time. "Good morning, Jane. And no, not especially," he said, still smiling. "Do *you* think you're crazy?"

I shrugged. "Yes. No. I don't know."

He leaned back in his chair and regarded me thoughtfully. I'd been pouring my heart out to him every Monday morning for nearly two years now, but I'd never flopped down onto the couch and demanded his take on my sanity.

I sighed. "You want me to talk about why I asked you that, but I don't know why. I just feel…sort of amped up."

"All right," he said gently. "So why don't you talk to me about that feeling?"

I opened my mouth and then shut it again. For once, I wasn't sure where to begin. I wanted to tell Dr. Jensen everything—that was what he was there for, right?

On the other hand, I didn't really want to admit my...recent extracurricular activities. Therapists might claim that they don't judge, but honestly: *everyone* judges.

Well, Dr. Jensen, I had a nooner at the Four Seasons, like it was some Hell's Kitchen flophouse.

Then I hit on some strangers.

And I kind of wanted to sleep with them.

Actually, take back "kind of."

He'd think I *had* gone crazy.

"I saw my sister over the weekend, and she tried to set me up with someone again," I said, shifting the subject—subtly, I hoped.

"And how did that make—"

"It made me feel annoyed," I said. Dr. Jensen had heard a lot about Mylissa over the years; such feminine perfection was a tough act to follow. "I don't know why she doesn't believe me when I say I don't want to date anyone."

"Why do you think that is, Jane?"

"Why don't you tell me?" I said, suddenly feeling ornery. "You're the expert in human behavior."

Dr. Jensen steepled his fingers together under his chin and gazed at me steadily. Affectionately, even. But he didn't answer the question.

I squirmed uncomfortably on his couch. I couldn't tell what he was thinking and it was driving me crazy.

I had the sudden and irresistible urge to fluster him. "Would you ever want to have sex with me?" I asked.

Dr. Jensen blinked rapidly. For the first time ever, I'd actually surprised him. But before he could answer, I backed off. "I'm kidding," I said. "Really. It was a joke."

Great—now I've got to get out of here, I thought.

Better to run away than explain why I'd asked him. Better to waste the appointment than admit to Dr. Jensen—and to myself, for that matter—that I probably had a crush on him.

Just a little one.

I was about to stand up, but then Dr. Jensen started to laugh—as if what I'd said was actually funny. He didn't say, *Why did you make that joke, Jane? Is this something we need to talk about?* Instead, he acted like I'd just told him the joke about the guy with the twelve-inch pianist.

Relief washed over me. I hadn't blown this—currently my only close relationship with someone of the opposite sex.

But, on the other hand, I wondered if Dr. Jensen ought to start talking to me about erotic transference or something. Didn't that seem like an obvious topic of conversation? *It is not uncommon for patients to experience romantic feelings for their therapist...* Blah, blah, blah.

Did Dr. Jensen know what I was thinking? If not, why was I paying him two hundred and fifty dollars a session?

I shook my head. I was obviously a little bit crazy.

Dr. Jensen was still smiling at me. Come to think of it, he'd been smiling at me the entire time I sat here.

And I had to wonder for real: *did* he want to sleep with me?

There was one way to find out.

But no, I wasn't *that* crazy.

Not yet.

CHAPTER 7

AFTER A WEEK OF begging, Brianne finally convinced me to go out with the brother of her current crush. A single date wasn't going to kill me, I reasoned, and since I'd just finished binge-watching *Homeland,* my Thursday evening was wide open.

And maybe, just maybe, I was a little bit lonely.

Nervously I approached Reynard: this would be my first date in six years. Then I saw the man who must be Nolan Caldwell waiting under the awning, eyes scanning the street.

He was very tall and slender, with black hair and eyes almost as dark. Every inch of him projected unwavering confidence, from the sharp jut of his chin to the expensive Italian loafers on his feet.

When he saw me, he hesitated. He looked me over carefully, like I was an expensive sweater he'd ordered off the Internet that he wasn't sure would fit.

Awkward.

"Nolan?" I said. "Hi, I'm Jane." I smoothed the shirred waist of the Dress nervously. "Jane Avery."

I must have passed his test, because he strode over to me and kissed my cheek, and then he gave me a dashing smile. "So good to meet you, Jane," he said, placing his hand at the small of my back. "Ready to go in?" But he was already steering me inside.

At a cozy corner table, Nolan reached for the wine list. "Not many Burgundies," he said, a note of reproach in his voice.

I had no response to that. If it was red and wine, I would probably drink it.

He eventually picked a bottle for us and said, "You're not vegetarian, are you?" He was ordering steak tartare before I'd shaken my head. "We'll share," he informed the waiter.

I looked at him in surprise. Who did he think he was, the CEO of blind dates? After he finished ordering things for me, would he ask me about synergy and leveraging my core competencies? Would he worry about his ROI for this fancy dinner?

As I sipped my wine—which was so expensive it practically tasted like money—I inspected him the way he'd inspected me. He was handsome, and obviously rich: two checks in the plus column. But on the minus side, he'd already racked up cocky, presumptuous, and snobbish.

"So how well do you know Brianne?" I asked.

"Never met her," he said.

"Oh," I said, surprised. "I guess I thought…" *I guess I thought she'd talk to a guy before she made me go out with him?*

"My brother and I don't run with the same crowd," Nolan said. "He's a gym rat. He even does MMA."

"Is that some kind of performance-enhancing drug?" I asked.

Nolan laughed—which surprised me, since he seemed deficient in the humor arena. "It stands for 'mixed martial arts.' Basically it amounts to rolling around on the floor with some muscular, sweaty, and half-naked meathead." He tucked his napkin into his lap as he shook his head in disapproval.

Hmmm, really? Rolling around on the floor with a muscular and sweaty half-naked…

"Jane?"

"Oh—what?" While my mind had seized that image and taken an R-rated run with it, Nolan was apparently still talking to me.

"I was asking if you liked the wine. I met the vintner last summer, when I vacationed in France."

"It's wonderful," I said. "I'd love to hear about the vineyard."

Nolan obliged me, as I'd guessed he would. Which meant that I was free to nod and smile…and to pay no attention at all to what he was saying.

Instead, I thought about Michael Bishop.

Actually, that's not right. I thought about the afternoon itself: the heat of Michael's hands, the tender urgency of his mouth, the sublime friction of skin against skin. There'd been no need to talk to each other because our bodies had known exactly what to do. Those hours, stolen from our regular lives, had been electric. I'd never felt that free before. That afternoon was a ten.

Or at least a nine.

I smiled to myself at the memory.

Nolan, of course, assumed that my expression was for whatever boring, pompous anecdote he was currently sharing, so he began to talk more loudly.

Let the cocky bastard think I care, I thought. *As soon I see the bottom of this wineglass, I'm out of here.*

And I was.

CHAPTER 8

I EDITED MICHAEL BISHOP'S article on the New York City Ballet the following morning. It didn't need much work; he was a great writer.

He was an even better kisser, though. And a truly memorable fu—

God, Jane! I shook my head to clear it. This was *ridiculous*. I needed to be thinking about *Metropolitan's* next issue, not replaying the afternoon with Michael for the two hundredth time, my body tingling at the still-vivid scenes.

I decided to take a walk; maybe the fresh air would restore my focus.

Stepping into the summer sunlight, I donned my big Burberry sunglasses and inhaled deeply. New York was beautiful today—the sky a brilliant sapphire, the clouds like enormous downy pillows. It was lunchtime, and people spilled out of office buildings all along Park Avenue South: women in floral dresses, men in button-downs and linen pants or dark tailored power suits.

I watched a cute, slightly scruffy guy fist-bump the doorman of his building, who grinned and said something that made the guy laugh. I could hear it from where I stood: a happy, infectious guffaw.

I was drawn to it. And, okay, I was also drawn to the guy's lean, athletic body.

When he started walking toward Madison Avenue, I followed him. He wore a plaid short-sleeved shirt and skinny jeans, and he sported a tattoo on each forearm.

I wondered if he had other, hidden ink and what it would look like.

I imagined unbuttoning his shirt and running my hands across his smooth chest. I thought about what it would feel like to touch those strong shoulders. I was deep in a delicious daydream when he stopped short—and I almost collided with his back.

I also nearly barreled into the pretty young woman who'd just come up and wrapped her arms around his waist.

He kissed her passionately on the mouth, and, arm in arm, they went to have lunch.

Or maybe they were hurrying off to have a nooner—which was obviously what I was looking for too.

So much for the walk clearing my mind!

But instead of heading back to the office, I kept walking toward Madison Square Park.

The Shake Shack line was a mile long, as usual. The benches lining the pathways sagged with the weight of people talking, reading, and eating takeout.

Not ten feet away sat a man on his lunch break, unwrapping a Shake Shack burger from its wax-paper sleeve.

He had sandy hair and high cheekbones, and he reminded me of someone I'd gone to high school with—a guy we'd voted most likely to become a TV weatherman.

He must have felt my gaze, because he looked up and gave me a curious half-grin.

I almost turned away—but I didn't. "You must've gotten in line at ten a.m. for that," I said, nodding at his lunch.

"Yeah, approximately," he agreed.

"So was it worth it?"

He looked at his burger thoughtfully. "I don't know yet." He held it out. "Want to try?"

"No!" I took a step backward, like he was about to force-feed me a sample.

"It was a joke," he said, grinning. "I don't share my lunch with strangers, even hot ones."

"No, of course not," I said, now feeling ridiculous. "That would be weird."

The irony didn't escape me: I'd been sizing him up for a nooner, but I wouldn't take a bite of his hamburger?

He nodded. "I like weird, but you gotta draw the line somewhere, right?" He took a bite. "Mmm. It's really good, though."

I sat down on the bench next to him. "Do you work around here?"

He gestured toward a stone building on the north side of the park. "In that one," he said. "You?"

"Over on Park Avenue South," I said. "I'm an editor at *Metropolitan* magazine."

"Cool, I have a subscription," he said. "I'm in grad school. Philosophy. Currently making ends meet as a marketing writer for a pet food company." He held out his fries, offering me a taste, and this time I took him up on it. They were hot, salty, and delicious.

"Have you seen that one where the dog goes, 'Your eyes are so beautiful. They're like meatballs'?" I asked. "I love that."

He looked at me proudly. "I wrote it."

I widened my eyes at him. "You're kidding. That billboard's in my subway stop!"

"Nope, not kidding," he said.

"You're obviously an unsung genius of promotional writing," I said. "Are you sure you want to keep studying Hegel or whoever?"

He grinned. "I'm in way too deep to ponder *that* philosophical conundrum," he said. "Which reminds me—" He glanced at his watch. "Shit, I've got to run to class." He got up, somehow simultaneously hurried and reluctant, and then he turned back to me. "You're a mad fox," he said. "I would love to get your number. But I'm sorry to say I'm engaged."

I gave him my best vamp's smile—which was also my first. "Are you sure your fiancée wouldn't let me borrow you, just for an afternoon?" I asked.

He looked shocked.

"I'm kidding," I said. "I don't have sex with strangers. Even hot ones."

Not yet, anyway, I thought as I watched him walk away.

This definitely wasn't what Bri had in mind when she urged me to get back in the game. Because this, honestly, was crazy.

But I didn't want to stop.

CHAPTER 9

"HOW'VE YOU BEEN, JANE?" Dr. Jensen asked as I settled into his overstuffed couch.

"Oh, I'm good," I said. "Everything's perfectly fine. Nothing to report. Life's totally, *completely* normal."

"Really? Well, I'm glad to hear that," he said. His tone conveyed what he really meant, which was *Tell the truth, Avery.*

But I still wasn't ready.

Did other women feel the way I did, though? Did they dream—and daydream—about getting it on, no strings attached? I really needed to know.

Luckily, there was an expert in these matters sitting right across from me. "Dr. Jensen, you must get told all kinds of secrets," I said.

"That's what I'm here for," he agreed. "Why they pay me the big bucks." He smiled.

"Tell me about it," I said, momentarily flashing on my none-too-large bank account. "I have a question for you. What do other women have to say about sex?"

His eyebrows nearly disappeared under his hair. I'd surprised him again.

"Look, sex used to be the only thing my friends and I ever talked about," I explained. "Who'd done it, and who they'd done it with. But now we've all grown up, and no one ever mentions it. Is it because we're adults and we've outgrown dirty secrets? Or is it just less exciting to talk about, now that we're not doing it in the back of our dad's station wagon? Not that *I* ever did that, mind you."

Dr. Jensen smiled thoughtfully. "What do you think, Jane?" he asked.

I groaned. "I don't care what I think," I said. "I want to know what other women tell you."

He hemmed and hawed, saying something about confidentiality and psychology's code of ethics.

I looked at him slyly. "Maybe you can't tell me because your clients don't feel comfortable enough to talk to you about that kind of thing," I said.

That was Manipulation 101, and Dr. Jensen knew it. "My clients tell me everything," he said.

I know one who doesn't, I thought. But I said, "Great! I want to hear about it."

"Jane, this is your time to talk about—"

"If it's my time, can't I use it the way I want?" I asked. "Sorry I interrupted you," I added.

Dr. Jensen looked at me carefully and seemed to come to a decision. "You understand I can't tell you anything that would allow you to identify another client. And everything I say is classified."

I snuggled deeper into the couch and mimed zipping my lips closed.

He took a deep breath. "All right, Jane. You asked for it, you got it. One of my clients talks about wanting to have sex with someone other than her husband." He paused. "And she wants her husband to watch."

"That's a tough thing to bring up over the salad course," I said.

"I have another client who's very wealthy," he said. "She's a patroness, and her life is one benefit luncheon after the other. Sex is only pleasurable for her if she's lying on fur." His eyes bored straight into mine. "Preferably lynx," he clarified.

"Because she's so rich?" *Kind of cliché,* I thought.

He shook his head. "Most of her life, she has to be as proper and poised as a marble Venus. The fur makes her feel both primitive and wild. It reminds her that she's an animal, too."

I was against fur—unless it was on a living mammal—but that almost made sense to me. "Can you tell me a fantasy in more detail?" I asked.

"Jane, again: this is your time to talk—"

"I think it would be therapeutic for me," I said. "Sorry, I interrupted you again."

He gazed out the window for a moment. Then he turned back to me and said, "All right. There's a woman I'll call Marie.

She likes to imagine that she has bound her breasts and disguised herself as a young man. In this costume, she finds work on a transatlantic ship. When another sailor catches her bathing and discovers her secret, she's terrified. He threatens to tell the captain unless she…pleases him. And so she does. At first it's against her will. But then she starts to enjoy it very much."

"Interesting," I whispered. This was a new one for me. Maybe I wasn't the only sex semimaniac in town.

"And then she ends up pleasing *many* of the sailors on the ship."

I felt myself blush. "That sounds…strenuous," I managed.

He said, "That's just the tip of Marie's iceberg."

"I'm listening," I said.

"I can tell," he said.

And for the rest of the session, I didn't say another word.

CHAPTER 10

IN SLING-BACKS AND MY black Dress, I inched my way through crowded, neon-lit Times Square. It was slow going, because I had a giddy eight-year-old on either side of me.

Grace, my niece, squeezed my hand happily. "I'm so glad you could come see *Aladdin* with us, Aunt Jane," she said. "Daddy was supposed to, but then he had a meeting."

I turned and gave Mylissa a mild but unmistakable little-sister scowl. "You told me this little Broadway adventure was a girls' night out," I said.

She glanced up from reapplying her scarlet lipstick. "What does it look like?" she asked.

"It looks like I'm here because your husband couldn't make it," I said.

"Ah, but *you could*," she said, blotting her lips with a tissue as we entered the theater.

"But—"

"I mean, really, Jane," my sister said. "Did you have something better to do?"

I sighed. Among Mylissa's many wonderful talents, there was also the unfortunate one of making me feel lame and inadequate.

It wasn't always this way: when I was married to James, with a two-bedroom in the Village and a new promotion at *Metropolitan,* my life had seemed enviable to her. It'd looked pretty great to me, too—until the day I caught James in our bed with Tracy, his ex, and everything fell apart.

The usher led us to our seats, which were excellent. One of the perks of having a brother-in-law with gobs of money, I guess.

Before the curtain rose, Grace laid her head on my shoulder. "Can we have a sleepover next weekend? Pleasepleaseplease?" she asked.

"Yes, may we, Aunt Jane?" said Charlotte, smiling prettily. She was the older twin by five minutes, and she liked everyone to know it.

I was flattered they wanted to spend the night in the city with me—and slightly chagrined that they, too, seemed to know I wouldn't have other plans.

"I love that idea," I said—and I really did mean it. "We can make popcorn and watch movies and paint our nails, and in the morning I'll make you blueberry pancakes with lots of syrup. Mylissa, what do you say?"

Mylissa turned to her daughters. "Your aunt *ought* to be going out on the weekends, girls," she said. "But she seems to relish her solitude."

"I don't know what that means," Grace said.

"It means she likes being alone," Charlotte translated.

"Yes, I do," I said. "But I like being with you two much better."

Mylissa crossed her arms. "If you'd only let me set you up with Jordan Andrews, Jane, you'd have dinner plans," she said. "Did I tell you he made partner?"

I kept my voice low and even. "I know you're trying to help, Mylissa. But like I said, it's really none of your business."

"Fine, if you want to be alone forever," she said huffily.

I was trying to be a good aunt by agreeing to host her darling children, and she was making me feel like a pathetic spinster: that didn't seem fair. But I kept my mouth shut because I didn't want to disagree in front of Charlotte and Grace, who were happily taking bets on whether or not there would be kissing in the musical and if, next weekend, I would let them watch two movies or three.

After a while, Mylissa turned to me and smiled sheepishly. "I'm sorry," she whispered over the top of Charlotte's head. "I shouldn't have said that about you being alone, and I'm sorry I didn't invite you first tonight. I'm *glad* it's you. Mike would just fall asleep."

I had to laugh, because she was right. Her husband worked an exhausting seventy hours a week: put him in a dark room and he'd sleep through the 1812 Overture, cannon fire and everything.

"I'm glad it's me too," I whispered back.

CHAPTER 11

WHEN WE LEFT THE theater, it was pouring rain. Mylissa and the girls gave me quick hugs and then dashed off toward the parking garage. I was left standing on the corner, soaked to the skin already.

It was impossible to get a cab in Times Square on a normal day—in a downpour, forget it. I'd have to make a mad dash for the subway.

"Upper West Side?" called a voice. From the backseat of a taxi, a man beckoned to me. "If you're going that way, we can share."

I squinted at him through the rain. He was in his fifties, with an open face and a deep cleft in his chin. He looked friendly, not to mention handsome, in a silver-haired, Richard Gere–ish sort of way.

I smiled because it reminded me of that scene in *Pretty Woman*—except that he wasn't driving a Lotus Esprit, and I wasn't a prostitute.

You've never slept with an older man before, Jane, I thought.

Then: *Keep your mind out of the gutter, Jane!*

"You're getting soaked," he pointed out.

Getting? I thought. I already looked like a drowned rat, albeit a well-dressed one.

"Last chance," the man called.

I dashed forward, shielding my face from the slanting rain with my knockoff Tory Burch tote. Sliding into the cab, I banged it against him, showering him with tiny, cold droplets. "I'm so sorry!" I exclaimed. "And thank you very much."

"No problem, I'll dry," he said good-naturedly. "You know, if you'd waited much longer, you probably could've swum home."

"It's at least three miles! I'm not Michael Phelps," I said, smiling.

"You're not? In that case I don't want to give you a ride after all." He grinned. "Hello, I'm Ethan Ross."

I shook his warm hand with my damp, chilled one. "Jane Avery," I said. I let my hand linger in his for a moment before pulling it away.

I gave the cabbie my address, and he drove wordlessly toward Eighth Avenue. The wheels hissed on the wet pavement, and the stoplights' reflections sparkled ruby and emerald against the black streets.

I felt much better now that I wasn't being deluged. Now that I was sitting next to a handsome man with a bare ring finger.

"It's actually a pretty night," I said to my cab-mate. "Assuming you've got a roof over your head, that is."

Ethan Ross peered out the window. "The city looks almost *clean*, so that's a minor miracle," he said.

"Yeah, and now I don't have to wash the car I don't have," I quipped.

He laughed, and then we sat in silence for a few blocks. It was a comfortable silence, but at the same time I worried he'd think I wasn't grateful for the ride.

I looked at him out of the corner of my eye.

He was looking at me too.

I flushed. Did Ethan Ross find me as attractive as I found him? Could a connection be that instantaneous?

There was one way to find out. I turned toward him, smiling. "Did you know that the average person will spend almost six months talking about the weather in his or her life?" I asked. Definitely not my best flirty line ever, but better than nothing.

"I had no idea," Ethan said, his eyes sparking with amusement. "Where'd you read that?"

"I don't remember," I admitted, "but after five years as a fact-checker, I'm a fount of trivial knowledge." I inched ever so slightly closer to him. I could smell his piney aftershave.

"Well, that's perfect, because I'm a big fan of random, useless facts," Ethan said, grinning. "What else do you have for me?"

I could feel his body heat warming the air between us. "Cab service dates back to the 1600s," I offered. I wanted to move still closer to him, but I restrained myself. "The cabbies drove carriages, of course, though I believe the proper term is *cabriolet*."

"Jane Avery, you're a very enlightening backseat companion." Ethan leaned toward me a little, and his knee brushed against mine. "So tell me, why are cabs yellow?"

"It's the color most easily seen from a distance," I said. "That's easy. Now you tell me something I don't know." I gave up on being subtle; I slid toward him until there wasn't any space between us at all. He inhaled sharply. "Maybe something about you," I said.

"I'd like to buy you a drink," he said, his mouth suddenly very close to mine. "You can tell me more trivia, and I'll find it fascinating. Honestly, you seem like the kind of woman who could make a lawn mower manual fascinating."

"Columbus and 89th," the cabbie said over his shoulder.

It was all up to me what happened next. I bit my lip, deciding. Then I nodded. "Yes," I said.

Ethan's hand cupped my cheek, a gesture so gentle it took my breath away. Then he turned to the cabbie and said, "Keep driving."

Ten blocks later, in the foyer of his apartment, Ethan Ross pulled me close and whispered, "Do you still want that drink?"

"I'll give you one guess," I purred, sliding the blazer from his shoulders.

"I'm going to guess no," he said, his lips suddenly soft but urgent against mine.

I wrapped my arms around his neck as we moved, our mouths still locked, into his bedroom.

The room was dark and I could barely make out a huge bed.

"Let's get you out of these wet clothes," he said, but I was way ahead of him: the Dress was already pooling at my ankles.

I fell backward onto the bed, pulling him on top of me. His weight felt delicious. His lips met mine with passion and tenderness. His hands caressed my breasts and he moaned.

"What do you want?" he whispered, planting thrilling kisses along my collarbone.

"I want you," I panted. "To—"

His fingers, somehow both urgent and gentle, were pulling down my panties. My mind seemed to be short-circuiting.

He smiled at me as he moved lower down my body, kissing every millimeter along the way. "You're so beautiful," he said. "Tell me what to do to please you."

His mouth on my stomach was warm and soft and wet. I was too breathless to answer. He looked up and grinned at me—a devilish, delighted grin—and then his head disappeared between my legs. His tongue found its target, and liquid fire shot through every nerve in my body.

"I want *that*," I gasped.

And things only got better from there.

CHAPTER 12

I WAS EXHAUSTED AT work the next day, but I didn't care. Everything about last night had been perfect—with the exception of the 3 a.m. cab ride home.

Hoping to avoid such an unpleasant necessity next time, I decided to set guidelines for my...*extracurricular activities*.

At the top of a blank page, I wrote TEN RULES FOR A RENDEZVOUS.

1. Do it at lunch—or possibly right after work. (Never neglect your beauty sleep.)
2. Scout out attractive prospects in the real world: no Tinder or Snapchat or whatever apps the kids are using these days.
3. No wedding rings. (Related: Look for tan lines of wedding rings quickly removed and pocketed.)
4. Swiftly approach the target and commence flirting.
5. Do not dawdle: efficiency and resolve are key.
6. Once mutual interest is confirmed, proceed to a neutral place (i.e., not his apartment or yours).

7. Orgasm must be achieved. (Yours.)
8. There is a time limit of 120 minutes.
9. No complications.
10. No second dates.

I looked my list over with a giddy thrill. It sounded so definitive—as if I really knew what I was doing.

"Jane!" Bri, her hands on her hips, was standing in the doorway. "Hello? I've been calling your name for like, *cinq minutes* at least."

"Oh, hi, Bri," I yelped, crossing my arms over my list. "What do you need?"

Bri gave me an odd look. "I don't *need* anything. I came by to say hi. What're you covering up?"

"Oh, nothing!" I said. "Just some ideas for the pitch meeting."

She raised a carefully penciled eyebrow at me. "Jane, are you hiding—"

Just then my phone rang, and I looked at the caller ID.

I'd never, *ever* been so happy to answer a call from my boss. "Hello, Jessica," I said. "I'll be right there."

Rolling her eyes at me, Bri moved away.

CHAPTER 13

AT EATALY, AN ENORMOUS, high-end Italian market not far from my office, there were dazzling displays of cured meats, gourmet cheeses, and heirloom fruits and vegetables. But the reason I'd walked in had nothing to do with soppressata or taleggio.

Every day, hundreds of men came here on their lunch hour.

Wearing a brand-new little black dress, I scanned the well-heeled crowd. I knew I could have my pick of these men. The knowledge made me feel decadent, like I'd stepped into Saks Fifth Avenue with a Birkin bag full of hundred-dollar bills.

Who would I select? Should I approach the dark-haired businessman reading the *Times*? What about the hipster in the scuffed Danner boots, or the man with tawny skin and perfect white teeth?

I didn't feel nervous about picking up a stranger—I felt powerful. I'd come a long way from the Four Seasons, that much was certain.

Over in the produce market, I spotted my target: a man in

a gray T-shirt and well-fitting jeans, with eyes the blue of a deep, glacial lake. Eyes I'd be happy to drown in.

I watched him select half a dozen persimmons, and as he carefully cupped the fruit I imagined those hands on my body. I thought about him pressing me up against the bins of melons, kissing me, not gentle anymore but hard and insistent—

I walked up to him and said, "Excuse me, can I ask you something?"

He turned toward me, and my stomach did a little somersault—his eyes were even more beautiful up close. "Sure," he said good-humoredly.

I picked up one of the rosy fruits and cupped it in my hand. "How can you tell if a persimmon is ripe?"

"Well, it depends on the type of persimmon," he said, happy to be able to help me. "This kind here, which is a Hachiya, has to be jelly-soft—otherwise it's like chewing a cotton ball."

"Okay, thanks," I said. "Can I ask you another question?" He nodded, and I dove right in. I said, "Would you like to spend the next hour or two with me? In a hotel room?"

I can't believe you just asked him that, Jane.

Half of me was scandalized; the other half was proud.

And the tiny part of me that said *This might be dangerous?* I completely ignored.

"Wow." He blushed, embarrassed, and ran his hand through his wavy brown hair. "Wow. Do you mean—"

"You know exactly what I mean," I said, handing him the persimmon. Then I gave him a smirk and headed toward the exit. I didn't need to turn around to know that he'd abandoned his groceries and was hurrying after me.

I took him to the Ace Hotel, to a cozy room decorated with vintage furniture and a splashy graphic mural. Not that it mattered: we only needed the bed.

But not right away, as it turned out.

We kissed our names into each other's mouths—his was Nick, or maybe Mick, I didn't want to take the time to clarify. I was hungry for him.

My hands had a mind of their own, greedily removing his T-shirt, then feeling the smooth slabs of muscle and warm skin underneath. His stubble scraped my lips and neck, and when his fingers found my nipples they caused a delicious, almost electric pain.

He wasn't embarrassed or flustered now. He knew exactly what he was doing. He whispered *"You want this, don't you?"* as he took my breast in his mouth. And when I said yes, his hands went under my dress, moved over my hips and ass, squeezing and rubbing them, and then his fingers slipped inside my black lace panties. He caressed me slowly at first, and then urgently, and as the pleasure grew I hung on to him so my trembling legs didn't collapse under me.

"Now turn around," he growled, pushing my hip with his free hand.

I let him spin me around and then I saw my face in the mirror: hair mussed, cheeks flushed, lips swollen from kissing. I saw him behind me, those beautiful, lustful eyes meeting mine in our reflection. I watched as he slid my dress up my legs and pushed it over my hips. I bent forward, put my hands on the desk. Then I saw him pull down the top of my dress and cup my breasts in his hands. He slid a finger into my mouth and I sucked it.

"You're amazing," he whispered.

I was almost breathless with desire, gasping how it was time, time for him to do what he came for.

I heard the scratch of the zipper on his jeans, the crinkle of the condom wrapper. Then I felt him, hot and hard, pressing against me. I pushed back, grinding myself against him.

And then with one thrust he was filling me. His fingers dug hard into my hips and I gripped the edge of the desk. The pleasure was so intense I couldn't think anymore—I could barely even see my own half-naked, sweat-slicked self in the glass. But I could hear the sound of bodies coming together again and again, and a gasping moan that must have been coming from my throat.

Afterward, my legs felt so weak I could barely stand. So when it was time to begin again, we collapsed onto the bed. I stared into those glacial eyes as he called my name and waves of ecstasy crashed over me. If drowning could ever be euphoric, this was what it would feel like.

Later, when he pressed his number into my hands, telling

me to *please, please call,* I slipped the little piece of paper into my pocket and told myself that it was okay to keep it.

There was something special about him—something wild but sweet, too.

Later, back at home, I unfolded the paper and smiled. *Nick Anderson,* he'd written. *Persimmon consultant.*

CHAPTER 14

ON FRIDAY, I TOOK the afternoon off and cabbed to the High Line, a narrow, elevated park on Manhattan's West Side. After treating myself to a gelato, I watched good-looking New Yorkers stroll along what had once been railroad tracks.

I hadn't been able to stop thinking about my trip to the Ace with Nick: the freedom and power I'd felt that afternoon was as good as the sex. Could I find that kind of pleasure again? Was it crazy to try?

Part of me thought I should quit while I was ahead. But that would be like putting my spoon down before I'd finished this fantastic, creamy *fior di latte,* which was so rich and delicious I shivered every time I took a bite.

I'd been celibate for sixteen months, hadn't I? That was a lot of sex not to have.

Still, maybe you should take a little break, Jane.

But what if I'm still having fun?

That was a good question. Then again, so was this: *What if I'm pushing my luck?*

When the young man with floppy blond hair and golden, sun-kissed skin sat down next to me, I took it as a sign from the universe.

As Bri would put it, I was still in the game.

"Sarah?" he asked, his voice sweet and uncertain.

I tipped up my hat and lowered my glasses. "I'm Jane," I said, smiling teasingly at him. "Who's Sarah?"

Confusion flooded his beautiful young face. He looked like Robert Redford in *Butch Cassidy and the Sundance Kid*— but younger and more fine-featured. "Um, she's my room-mate's girlfriend. I thought…" He frowned lightly. "Did we meet at Noah's party? If so, I'm sorry—I was kind of drunk."

"We haven't met until right this instant," I said. I put a spoonful of gelato in my mouth, pulled it out slowly, and licked suggestively at the spoon.

His eyes widened. He held out his hand. "I'm Jake," he said.

I took his hand, and, still holding it, I stood up. "Would you like to take a walk with me, Jake?" I nodded toward the gleaming Standard Hotel, which straddled the High Line a few blocks south.

He practically leapt off the bench.

Luckily, the hip hotel had a room for us, with a floor-to-ceiling view of the Hudson River and the blue summer sky.

Jake, who'd been chattering nervously for the last ten min-utes, now stood in the middle of the room—the way I had, weeks ago, with Michael Bishop—silent and awed.

I stepped up to him and put my hands on his perfect cheeks. "You're going to like this very much," I said reassuringly. "Now kiss me."

He obeyed, awkwardly at first, but he got better fast.

I put his hands on the zipper of my dress and helped him slide it down. "And now my bra," I whispered.

His expression was desire tinged with doubt—as if he thought that at any moment, he might wake up in his tiny apartment with the realization that this was nothing but an incredible dream.

I put his hands on my breasts and he sucked in his breath and said, "Ohhh—"

"Now take off your clothes," I said softly, and I smiled as he obeyed.

I admired his lean body, with its small patches of downy gold hair: his hard, flat stomach, his long legs, his smooth arms. I pulled him toward me and nuzzled his neck.

"I've never done this before," he said, wonder in his voice.

"Had sex with an older woman?" I said, grinning lasciviously. "A MILF?"

Flustered, he blinked rapidly. "No, I mean—"

I laughed. "I don't have children, so I'm not a MILF."

"I meant…" he said. "I meant that I haven't…hooked up with someone like this."

"Mmm, me either," I murmured.

It wasn't a lie, because I'd never hooked up with anyone I met on the High Line before.

I led him to the bed. He followed, eager as a puppy.

He lay back and I bent over him, kissing his chest and stomach. Then, after teasing him for a while, I took him in my mouth.

His hands gripped the sheets. "Oh God," he gasped. "I love you, I love that."

I smiled as best I could.

When I mounted him, easing my body up and down as he gripped my hips, I felt wild, charged with thrilling life. Every nerve sang as he bucked beneath me. I closed my eyes and threw my head back and abandoned myself to the bliss.

When I collapsed on top of him, exhausted, he wrapped his arms around my damp back.

He kissed my neck, my cheeks, the palms of my hands. "Thank you," he said sweetly.

I laughed. "No, thank *you,*" I said.

CHAPTER 15

"THAT'S A NICE SCARF you're wearing," Dr. Jensen said as I flopped down in my usual spot.

"Thanks," I said, touching the blue silk at my neck. I was wearing it to hide the hickey the Sundance Kid had given me. "I don't think you've ever complimented me before."

Smiling, Dr. Jensen shrugged. "It's not typically a therapist's role. But that's a good color on you. It matches your eyes."

Is my therapist flirting with me?

I was probably just being crazy again. Well, if so, I was in the right place for it.

"Have you seen Marie lately?" I asked, leaning back against the cushions and trying to sound casual.

Dr. Jensen did his best to look stern. "Jane, I don't think we should keep talking about other clients' fantasies anymore when we really ought to be talking about you."

He had a point, of course. I sighed. Maybe I *shouldn't* pretend I was still the Jane Avery I used to be: lonely, celibate, and addicted to Netflix. Maybe I should acknowledge who—or what—I'd become.

Not that there was a word for it. If I were a guy, I'd be a player. But what term existed for a woman like me? Sex goddess? Too cheesy. *Demimondaine?* Only Bri would know what it meant. An erotically empowered woman who played by her own rules? That took way too long to say.

Dr. Jensen leaned forward. "What are you thinking, Jane?"

"Do you know how long it takes to get over a divorce?" I asked suddenly.

Dr. Jensen rubbed his nose, right where his glasses would be if he ever wore them. He said, "There's no magic number of months or days."

"Actually, there is," I said, sitting up straighter. *"Sixteen and a half months."* I realized this only as I said it, but it was true. "I'm finally over the heartbreak, Dr. J. Finally over James and what he did to me. To us."

I knew I looked shocked, giddy. And I almost couldn't believe it: I hadn't longed to have James beside me in bed for weeks now. Hadn't felt broken by his betrayal. Hadn't wondered if he regretted throwing everything we had away.

I'd been too busy having the kind of fun I didn't think a good girl like me could ever have.

"I can't tell you how happy I am to hear that," Dr. Jensen said. "But this seems like a rather sudden shift. Did something happen?"

A lot *of things happened,* I thought, pressing my thighs together as an image of naked Nick tumbled through my mind.

"You know what they say," I chirped. "Time heals all wounds!"

"I get the sense there's something you're not telling me," Dr. Jensen said.

I stared down at my hands because I didn't want to meet his gaze. I couldn't admit anything to him yet, but nor was I willing to lie. "I've been doing some…emotional work on my own," I said. "I mean, in addition to what we've been doing here," I added. I didn't want him to feel he wasn't helping me.

"I'd like to hear about it," he said.

Yeah, well, I'd like to hear about Marie and her sailors, I thought, suppressing a smile that threatened to give me away. *Looks like neither of us is going to get what we want today.*

"Jane?" he asked.

"I'm not quite ready," I said honestly.

And honestly, I wondered if I ever would be.

He nodded. "Okay, I understand. I'm here for you when you are."

"I know," I said. "I'm glad I have someone like you. No, scratch that. I'm glad I have *you.*"

I could have sworn he blushed.

CHAPTER 16

HAVE LUNCH WITH ME today, the text from James read. *Gramercy Tavern, noon.*

I stared at my phone in shock. For one thing, James and I hadn't spoken in four months. For another, the Gramercy Tavern was romantic and expensive: in other words, not the kind of place you take your ex.

Maybe James had somehow sensed that I was over him, and he'd decided to win my heart back.

Then he'd probably rip it out and stomp all over it, just like he did last time.

Well, there was no way I was going to let that happen. I wasn't that kind of girl anymore.

So I texted him back. *See you at 12:15.*

Then I smiled to myself. This lunch was going to be *interesting*.

James was already at the table when I arrived, and my heart gave a tiny lurch when I saw his familiar, handsome face. Dark, intense eyes, full, sensual mouth—and a girl could cut glass on those cheekbones.

Okay, maybe I *wasn't* entirely over him.

He stood and kissed me, just a millimeter from my lips. "You look magnificent, Jane," he said, letting his hand linger at my waist. "Have you been working out?"

Yes, but not at a gym. "I've been walking on the weekends," I said—which was partially true.

He pulled out my chair and then poured us glasses of rosé. "It's really, *really* good to see you," he said, his eyes still sweeping over my arms, my chest, my face.

"You too," I said, pretending not to notice his admiring gaze. I'd worn a low-cut dress after all. "It's been a long time. What's new?"

His expression quickly darkened. "Tracy and I broke up," he said.

"Again?" I said drily. She'd been his ex before I was. It was stumbling upon the two of them in flagrante delicto—in other words, she was riding him like a rodeo stallion—that had led to our divorce.

"For the last time, though," James said.

"I'm sorry to hear that." And I meant it too.

"It's for the best, really," he said. "What about you? Are you seeing anyone?"

"Me? Oh, no," I said. "No, no, no." I took a gulp of wine. *The lady doth protest too much, methinks.*

"But you've been dating," he said.

"Nope," I said. I flashed him a big smile. "No interest!"

"Oh," he said, sounding surprised. "But you just seem

so—I would've thought—I mean, look at you—" He floundered.

"How's the mutt?" I interrupted, because if I couldn't talk about my sex life with my therapist, I certainly wasn't going to try it with my ex-husband.

James sighed. "He gets into so much trouble he must think his name is No, Boy! But I love him to pieces." Then James shot me a look I could only describe as mischievous. "How's the cactus?" He grinned like he already knew the answer.

Which he did.

"Gone to the great desert in the sky," I admitted.

He shook his head affectionately. "Oh, Jane," he said.

"Don't 'Oh, Jane' me." I laughed. "You can't even put your oxford on right."

He looked down. "Oops."

As James discreetly unbuttoned his shirt in order to fix it, I remembered how I used to watch him undress before getting into bed. How his chest was perfectly smooth and hairless until right above the waist of his boxers. How he'd do a sexy little hip shimmy just to make me laugh.

When we were first married, we did it every night—and half the mornings too.

I crossed my legs under the table, trying to ignore the tingling I felt between them. *This is lunch, Jane, not a booty call.*

Right?

The waiter glided over and gave us a minuscule bow. "To

start, we have the beef carpaccio with a broccoli rabe pesto," he intoned.

"I ordered the tasting menu—is that okay?" James asked as the platter of thinly sliced meat was set down between us.

"Perfect," I said, my mouth already watering. "Did you know that carpaccio is named after the Italian painter Vittore Carpaccio? The red-and-white tones of his paintings reminded people of raw meat."

James shook his head and smiled. "You always know the weirdest stuff," he said. "I loved that about you."

The meat was so tender it melted in my mouth. "Thanks," I said. "And oh my God, *this is delicious.*"

"I always loved to watch you eat too," James said, sounding almost shy.

"Now you're just embarrassing me," I said, ducking my head. "Also—why?"

He shrugged. "You really appreciate good food, and you look so happy when you eat it. It's…I don't know. Charming. And sexy."

I put my fork down. What was going on here? "James," I began.

He blushed and looked uncomfortable. "I'm sorry. Forget I said anything. I was trying to pay you a compliment. Maybe…maybe now isn't the time."

But what was my rule again? *If life hands you a compliment, take it.*

I said, "If you think I look good eating carpaccio, wait until we get to the chocolate semifreddo with the salted caramel sauce."

James laughed. "I can't wait." His hand crept toward mine across the table.

But we didn't touch.

As the waiter brought us plate after plate of phenomenal food—ricotta tortellini, roasted duck breast—James hardly ate. He just watched me.

I knew exactly what he was thinking, because I was thinking it too.

His apartment was a five-minute cab ride away. We could race over there, pawing at each other in the backseat, and we could rush upstairs and fall into that king-sized bed of his. And there we could do what we'd done best.

It sounded better than dessert.

"I miss you," James said softly.

I smiled. "I miss you too," I said.

I knew that going back to his apartment would be like going back in time. Everything would be just as it had been—except for me.

I was totally different.

He reached farther across the table and finally took my hand. "Do you think…"

I let him hold my hand for a moment, and then I pulled it away. "Missing isn't a feeling you have to fix," I said softly. "It's something we can live with. We had a good thing for a while. We don't anymore. And I'm finally okay with that."

CHAPTER 17

JANE, YOU IDIOT, THIS *isn't how it's supposed to work!*

I paced back and forth across my parquet floor until my downstairs neighbor knocked a broom handle against his ceiling.

"Sorry!" I called down. "Stopping now!" Then I sank down onto the couch and tried to calmly consider my situation.

I had managed to turn down my ex-husband. But I had kept Nick's number—and, more important, I'd used it. I'd gone so far as to ask him to meet me on the steps of the Met, tonight at 7 p.m.

Yes, the sex had been amazing. But it was the "persimmon consultant" that got me. It was both goofy and sly—a combination I found irresistible.

I imagined us having a glass of champagne on the museum's balcony bar, high above the Great Hall, laughing, talking, and getting to know each other (with our clothes on). Then we'd stroll through Central Park, dodging Rollerbladers and bikers as we made our way toward the Conservatory Garden to admire the last of the tulips. We'd hold hands. We'd kiss under the wisteria-covered pergola.

It sounded like a perfect date.

The problem was, second dates were absolutely *against the rules.*

I glanced over at the *Dress,* tossed carelessly on the back of my reading chair. It was the only witness to the secret life I'd been living, and I desperately wished I could ask it for advice.

I thought of Nick's gorgeous eyes and his infectious laugh. Because he was *funny*—I'd learned that later, when we lay curled on the bed, his hand resting tenderly on my hip as he told me stories of his reckless youth.

He could be serious too. *I've never met anyone like you,* he'd said. *You thrill me.*

He had thrilled me too.

So what was I supposed to do? I looked at the clock; it was 6:50 p.m.

I imagined Nick already waiting for me on the steps, dodging tourists' feet as they heaved themselves up the stairs, shooing away the pigeons hunting for scraps, and scanning the crowd for a tall brunette in black.

Soon he'd start checking his phone. Start wondering where I was.

His fingers itching to touch me again.

I grabbed my purse and dashed out the door.

But instead of heading east toward the museum, I turned in a different direction.

CHAPTER 18

"JANE-*ITSA!*" AL SAID, leaning across the counter to give me a paternal kiss on the cheek. "You hungry?"

"No, thanks, Al," I said. My heart was pounding. To make it to the Met on time, I'd need a hovercraft to float over the rush-hour traffic. "I just came in for a quick coffee."

I put two dollars down on the Formica, and almost immediately, Veta appeared with a steaming cup, swirling with cream the way I liked it.

"Here you go, sweetie," she said, patting my shoulder. "You look extra pretty again. But I'm not going to say anything!" She clapped her hands over her mouth, but I heard muffled words that sounded a lot like "I hope you have a date."

Yes, Veta, I do have a date, I thought. *I have a date with someone I could actually fall for. And* that *is the problem.*

A big clock, the kind they have in every high school classroom, hung above the doorway to the kitchen. As I watched, the minute hand lurched forward with an audible click.

I felt my pulse quicken.

Rule #10. No second dates.

Don't do this, Jane.

I got up from my stool.

"Where are you going, Janie?" Veta called. "You forgot your change. Do you need a to-go cup?"

I strode out to the sidewalk where I stood, jittery with nerves, under the blue-and-white awning that said AL'S #1 DINER. When Nick answered his phone on the second ring, I said, "I can't make it tonight. I'm really sorry."

"What's the matter?" he asked, sounding worried. "Is everything all right?"

Yes, I thought. *No.*

"Everything's fine. I just—I just can't do it."

There was a silence on the other end of the line. Then Nick said, "I don't understand."

I didn't want to say it again, but I had to. "I can't go on a date with you."

"You mean you don't want to," he said.

"It's not that I don't want to," I admitted. "It's that I can't."

"Why not?" he asked. "Are you married or something?"

He couldn't see my rueful smile or the shake of my head. "Not anymore."

"Okay, well, have you been kidnapped? Are you tied up in a basement somewhere in Queens? Do you need mad ransom money? Because I've got it. Tell me where you are and I'll be right there with a suitcase full of cash."

I laughed. "I'm free," I said.

"Then come be with me," he said, his voice now low and urgent.

A teenage couple came staggering up the sidewalk toward me, the boy carrying the girl piggyback, both of them laughing hysterically. Behind them, an old man and an old woman walked slowly arm in arm, their heads bent close together.

And then there was me, alone.

And *fine with it.*

I steeled myself. "For the fifth time—or maybe the millionth, I've lost track—I just can't see you tonight," I said. "I'm sorry."

"Then another night," Nick said. "Tomorrow or the next night or the next."

He was starting to sound desperate, which was kind of sweet.

"It doesn't work that way—" I began. But then I stopped. What was I going to say? I knew I couldn't explain it to him. *I slept with you, and it was fantastic, and I might really like you—but I absolutely won't have dinner with you.*

He just wouldn't understand.

I didn't know if I did either.

"Jane, we really had something," Nick said softly.

"We sure did," I agreed. "And I'll never forget it."

And then I hung up the phone.

CHAPTER 19

THE DOOR TO THE Red Room was tucked away under scaffolding, not to mention totally unmarked. When I finally spotted it, I took a deep breath.

Am I really about to do this?

A laughing, good-looking couple brushed past me and entered, arms wrapped around each other. I craned my neck but couldn't see inside. Suddenly uncertain, I paced the sidewalk in my satin shift that put the *little* in *little black dress,* and wondered if I had finally and completely lost my mind.

A handful of fun trysts wasn't such a big deal, not in the grand scheme of things. Tonight, though, was something else entirely.

I, Jane Aline Avery, was about to go into a sex club.

I could feel my pulse pounding all the way down into my fingertips.

I felt exhilarated. And *miles* beyond nervous.

Maybe, just maybe, things were getting out of control.

A moment later, the unmarked door opened again, and

the good-looking couple reappeared, beckoning to me. "Come on in, gorgeous," the woman said, smiling. "Don't be scared!"

I blushed, tried to stand still. "Is it that obvious?" I asked.

Her dark-haired date nodded. "You look like a kitten at the door of the dog pound, sweetie. But there's nothing to worry about. Come in with us! We'll take care of you."

I didn't even have time to answer before the woman reached out and took my hand. Her touch was delicate—and strangely reassuring.

"I'm Sasha," she said, "and this is David. We're regulars." She gave my hand a gentle squeeze.

Surprised, I smiled back at her. She seemed nice, and also perfectly normal—not a scary sex maniac. Maybe the Red Room wasn't so different from a dance club, I thought. And so, after only a moment's hesitation, I let her lead me inside.

Yes, I was really going to do this.

Candles flickered in the lobby, their light reflected in gilt-framed mirrors. To my left were a bar and a dance floor; to my right, a big room with an enormous wall-to-wall bed.

"Give it an hour," Sasha told me, nodding toward the empty mattress. "Then that'll be *writhing* with naked flesh."

I gulped. *Maybe, on second thought…*

Sasha grinned as she pulled me toward the bar and ordered us Kir Royales. "Don't worry," she said. "Everything's going to be great. And remember: you don't have to do anything you don't want to do."

But what *did* I want to do? That was the million-dollar question.

I watched a half-naked woman spin acrobatically around a pole while Sasha gave me a good-natured mini-lecture about the absurdity of sexual monogamy. David interjected with helpful information about the club, including the location of the locker rooms, the dungeon, and the late-night buffet.

"No sex near the food," he informed me. "That's pretty much the only rule."

I nodded as if none of this were surprising, but my stomach was doing somersaults.

Suddenly an attractive forty-something man was by my side, his hand on my arm. "Smile if you want to make out with me," he said.

I took a step back in alarm—this was *way* too soon.

He read my expression immediately, said, "Okay then, have a good night," and vanished.

"Whoa," I said, turning back to Sasha. "What just happened?"

"We take *no* very seriously around here," she explained. "A girl can't have fun if she doesn't feel safe."

"That's a relief," I said. I took a sip of my drink, hoping to calm my nerves. "And I obviously didn't break his heart." I pointed to the corner, where he was already making out with a pretty young redhead wearing a vinyl nurse's outfit and carrying a riding crop.

Sasha laughed and patted my hand. "I'm so glad we found you," she said. "You're a unicorn, you know."

"What does that mean?"

"It means a single girl who wants to swing," David answered. His arm curled around my shoulders—but it felt friendly, not creepy. "Do you want to go upstairs?"

I was as rare as a mythical beast? Feeling suddenly giddy, I said, "Why not?"

On the second floor, everything was red: red candles, red lightbulbs, red pedestals bearing red bowls of condoms.

Oh—and there was a couple having sex on a red leather couch not five feet away from where I stood.

This is out of control, said the voice in my head. *You are out of control.*

The couple's moans of ecstasy carried over the music.

Sasha and David watched them avidly for a moment, and they weren't the only ones enjoying the show. A topless woman stepped forward and leaned down toward them, and the woman on the couch began to kiss her breasts as the man ran his hand over her black leather skirt.

"What do you think?" Sasha asked, smiling at me.

"I don't know," I said honestly. "It's a little…overwhelming?"

Sasha linked her fingers through David's and nodded toward a small room furnished with a normal-sized bed and an armchair. "Want to come play?" she asked me. "Or, if you want to ease into it, you can just watch."

I was flattered by their attention, and I actually liked them. But I didn't think I was a voyeur or a two-at-once type. I smiled and shook my head. "Thanks, but you guys go ahead," I said. "I'm going to, uh, keep looking around."

"Okay. You know where to find us," Sasha said. She leaned forward and surprised me with a soft, Kir-flavored kiss. "See you later, I hope."

I noticed they left the door to their room open.

Alone, still feeling the sweet tingle of Sasha's kiss, I fidgeted nervously. Was this a huge mistake?

There was really only one way to know. I tossed back the rest of my drink, straightened my shoulders, and scanned the room. I saw a man with his hands down a woman's tiny disco shorts and two naked girls fondling each other on a table. Low bass thudded in the background, and it seemed like there were more pheromones in the air than there was oxygen.

I caught the eye of a tall, dark-haired man standing near one of the private rooms. I sucked in my breath.

His gaze was so intense it was like a physical touch.

I stared back without smiling, letting the tension between us build. Then, feeling bolder, I beckoned him over.

"You're new here, aren't you," he said, giving me a sexy half-smile.

"How can you tell?" I asked, trying to sound playful. He was so tall that my head didn't even come up to his shoulders.

"You look as freaked out as I did an hour ago. I'm Dylan."

When he brought my hand to his lips and kissed it, a tiny jolt of electricity shot through me. "And you are?"

"Jane, and I do not look freaked out," I insisted.

"Really," he said, unconvinced. "Then let's see how you look now." And, still holding my hand, he pulled me into the dungeon.

It was a large, dark room with dripping candles mounted in iron sconces. I saw paddles, switches, and whips, some resting on hooks and some in use. In the middle of the room hung some kind of elaborate harness, with a pale, naked girl writhing ecstatically in it. Another woman, naked except for her thigh-high boots, cracked a whip near the girl's legs.

All right, I probably looked freaked out now.

But I was turned on by this man, by his coal-hued eyes and his long-fingered hands. By the animal energy that seemed to shimmer from his smooth skin.

"What do you think?" he asked, giving me a tiny smirk.

I shrugged, all put-on nonchalance. "Whips aren't really my thing. But whatever anyone else does is their business, right?"

"To each his own," he agreed. He stepped closer to me. "Or her own." His fingertip brushed my bottom lip—a touch impossibly light, yet I felt it in every nerve.

The girl in the sling moaned as the woman dragged the whip along her skin. Someone began blowing out candles, and the room grew darker and seemingly hotter.

I told myself that no one here mattered but me and

this gorgeous man. I said, "Smile if you want to make out with me."

He flashed me a beautiful grin, and then he kissed me. Hard. My hands slid around his waist as I pressed my body against his. He broke the kiss before I was ready, taking an ice cube from his drink and putting it in his mouth, then bending down to my neck. The heat and the cold, the tease of his tongue—they made me shiver and gasp.

But when he reached for the zipper on my dress, I put my hand on top of his. "No, no, not here," I said.

"Then tell me where," he whispered.

CHAPTER 20

WE CABBED TO MY apartment, and we'd barely gotten inside before Dylan had me up against the wall, his hands strong and urgent on my body.

I was breaking a major rule, bringing him home, but I didn't care. I'd crossed so many lines already—what was one more?

Summer heat lightning flashed outside the window, illuminating my cluttered living room. Dylan was the first man I'd ever had in my apartment, but he didn't see the mess of books and magazines and coffee mugs. He cared about nothing but me.

"I'm going to bend you over the couch," he said into my neck. "But not just yet."

"What are you going to do first?" I whispered, thrilled.

Before tonight, I'd been the one in charge—but here was a man who wanted to be in control. It was electrifying.

And just a little bit scary.

His hands squeezed my ass, hard, and he said, "Don't talk."

I groaned as he ground his hips into me, a taste of what was to come.

"Not yet," he said again. Then he grabbed my wrists and yanked them down. He held them both in one big hand, tight behind my back, as his tongue traced the seam of my lips and then pushed into my mouth.

It was a hungry, ravaging kiss, and it left me breathless.

"First," he said, "the bed." And then he picked me up and carried me into my room.

I, who hadn't felt small since I was ten, felt tiny in his powerful arms. He set me down, pulled off my dress and everything else in a matter of seconds, and then pushed me back onto the down comforter.

I felt a sense of vertigo as he knelt between my legs, still clothed.

Excitement tinged with a kind of exquisite fear: my heart beat faster and faster. His desire had a violent edge, I could sense it. But I didn't want to stop.

He reached into his back pocket and pulled out a silk scarf, and before I'd even processed what was happening he was winding it around my wrists and whispering, "That's a good girl, you're going to like this."

When he had both of my arms tied to the bedpost, he licked his way down my body as his hands pinched my nipples. I arched up and pressed myself into his mouth.

It didn't matter that I couldn't move—I didn't want to move. I only wanted him to keep doing what he was doing. My powerlessness excited me.

But then suddenly he slipped the silk from my wrists, and

in one quick, fluid motion he flipped me over so I was on my hands and knees. I turned back to look at him and saw him pull his hand back. Before I could tell him to stop, his palm connected with my hip and a red, stinging pain shot through me. I gasped in shock.

"You like that?" he asked, his voice husky.

"I don't know!" I cried. I did and I didn't. It scared me.

His fingers slid between my legs and found the wetness there. "I'm sorry, Jane," he whispered. One hand caressed me—and the other delivered another slap.

I cried out. He was testing my limits. I didn't know where they were myself, pleasure mixing with pain, desire with doubt.

Lightning flickered again and I saw him taking off his jeans. "I'll try to be gentle," he said.

"Yes," I gasped.

When he pushed into me, not gentle at all but forceful, animalistic, I couldn't tell if the flash of light was in my mind or outside my window. I felt like I was shattering. It was amazing and it was terrible—

But what was that glint of *metal* I could see, half hidden under his discarded jeans?

In a rough whisper, he said, "Now we're going to try something different."

I think I might have made a big mistake.

CHAPTER 21

THE PHONE SEEMED TO ring forever before voice mail finally picked up.

"You have reached Jane Avery. Sorry, I'm not available to take your call right now. Here comes the beep. You know what to do."

Jessica Keller, publisher of *Metropolitan* magazine, slammed the phone down in frustration. Actually, she *didn't* know what to do.

Jane—reliable, punctual, hardworking Jane—was three hours late for work.

Without her, the Friday-morning edit meeting had dissolved into gossip and bickering. None of the staff writers had met their deadlines, and the fact-checkers, given no new articles to review, were staring glassy-eyed at Facebook or playing computer solitaire.

Until today, until *right this very second,* Jessica hadn't realized how desperately she needed her second-in-command.

And, though she had called her twenty times at least, Jane wasn't picking up her phone.

Agitated, Jessica strode down the hall to Brianne Delacroix's office. The petite redhead was talking animatedly into her headset about "buttressing circulation in order to make rate base."

Jessica made a slicing motion across her chin, and Bri quickly ended her call.

"Is everything okay?" Bri asked, standing up and smoothing her skirt nervously.

Jessica snapped, "Have you heard from Jane?"

Bri's eyes widened. "No," she said. "I texted her last night, but—"

"Did you hear back?" Jessica interrupted.

Bri shook her head. "No."

The two women stared at each other.

"Maybe she took a sick day," Bri whispered. "And she forgot to call in."

"Jane is the most responsible person I know," Jessica said. "That is not the kind of thing she'd ever forget to do."

Bri grew pale. Jessica clenched and unclenched her hands. *Where in the world was Jane Avery?*

CHAPTER 22

"JANE, YOU'D BETTER NOT be screening me, you wench," Mylissa said into her headset—half laughing, half annoyed. "Are the girls coming for a sleepover tomorrow night or what? Mike's in Toronto on business, so can I come too? I promise not to mention Jordan Andrews, or say anything at all about your pitiful social life. Whoops! Sorry, don't be mad. What I meant to say was your, um, *selective* social life. Quality over quantity, right? Like shoes. Speaking of which, I came into the city today and I'm about to buy the most amazing pair of Stuart Weitzman heels—seriously, you'll *die* when you see them."

Mylissa was well on her way to a ten-minute voice mail when another call came in and she clicked over. "Hello?"

"Who is this?" demanded an unfamiliar voice.

"Excuse me?" Mylissa asked, bristling. "Who are *you?*"

"This is Jessica Keller. I'm Jane's boss, and this is the number she listed as an emergency contact."

Mylissa gasped. "I'm her sister. What's wrong? Is she

okay?" Her heart began to thud painfully in her chest, and she gripped the shoe rack to steady herself.

"I don't know," Jessica said. "She's not at work and she's not answering her phone. This is completely and totally unlike her."

Mylissa dropped the Weitzman heels and began running toward the Barneys exit. She flagged down a cab and threw herself into the back, breathlessly giving Jane's address and telling him to hurry, hurry, it was an emergency.

"Hello? Hello?" Jessica's muffled voice came from the pocket of Mylissa's handbag, but Mylissa didn't even notice.

All she could think about was her baby sister and what terrible thing must have happened to her.

CHAPTER 23

BARELY TEN MINUTES LATER, Mylissa was pounding on the super's ground-floor door and yelling at the top of her lungs.

Superintendent R. J. Dattero, obviously roused from a midmorning nap, stuck his disheveled head out the window and looked at her in confusion. "Can I help—"

"Let me into my sister's apartment," Mylissa demanded. "Jane Avery. Three A."

R.J. continued to stare, unmoving, until Mylissa's patience snapped. "Wake up!" she cried, stamping her foot the way her daughters did. "Jane's in trouble."

Saying it, Mylissa knew she was right, and her mind whirled with awful possibilities. Jane had fallen in the shower and knocked herself unconscious. She'd cut herself on a knife and was slowly bleeding out on the linoleum.

I was too hard on her, Mylissa thought. *I'll never forgive myself.*

R. J. Dattero finally mobilized and came outside. Pulling a ring of keys from his pocket, he opened the building's front door and began arthritically climbing the narrow staircase to Jane's apartment. Mylissa had to fight the urge to scream at him or even push him upward—*anything* to make him go faster.

Potential disasters continued to present themselves. *Jane contracted E. coli from that Greek diner she loves so much, and her kidneys are failing. She drank too much and got alcohol poisoning. She had a heart attack.*

When R.J. unlocked the door of 3A, Mylissa shoved him out of the way and burst into the living room.

Panic exploded in her chest like a bomb, dimming her vision, deafening her to R.J.'s shout of shock.

Clothes were strewn everywhere. A footstool was knocked over. Spilled wine, dark as blood, puddled on the hardwood floor.

Mylissa thought she'd prepared herself for what might have gone wrong.

But never in a million years could she have predicted the scene before her.

In the middle of all that mess, Jane, her baby sister, was kneeling by the radiator.

Naked.

Chained to it by a pair of handcuffs.

Mylissa rushed over and flung herself to the floor in front of her sister. "Janie, Janie, what happened?" she cried. "Were you robbed? Where are your clothes? Did someone hurt you?"

Meanwhile, she tried to cover Jane with her shawl so R.J. wouldn't see her bare and trembling limbs. "Go get bolt cutters!" she cried over her shoulder. "Hurry, you comatose old dinosaur!"

Jane was laughing and crying at the same time, mascara leaving black lines down her cheeks. "I'm fine, I'm fine," she insisted. "I wasn't robbed. I wasn't raped. Oh God, I'm so glad to see you, Mylissa." She sniffled, hiccupped, giggled. "You can't call Mr. Dattero a dinosaur, that's not nice."

Mylissa took her sister's face in her hands. "What the hell is going on, Janie?" she asked. "I was so worried! I thought you were dead. And thank *God* you're not, but why are you chained to a radiator?"

Jane tried to look away, and Mylissa watched as she grew bright crimson.

"Seriously. You'd better start talking," Mylissa said.

Jane heaved an enormous sigh and tried to meet her sister's gaze. "You always say I don't have a social life," she eventually said. "But I do, actually. And this…well, this is what you might call a side effect of it."

"I don't understand," Mylissa said.

"I brought a man home," Jane said. "And—" She stopped and glanced over to the door. R.J. had returned.

Mylissa leapt up, snatched the bolt cutters from his hands, and shoved him back into the hall.

"Actually," Jane began, "I don't think you need those. The key—"

But Mylissa was already hacking her way through the chain. "There!" she cried triumphantly as the metal gave way.

Released, Jane stood, the cuff still dangling from her wrist like a bracelet. Then she raced out of the room.

"Jane!" Mylissa cried. *What was going on?*

A moment later, Jane reappeared in a bathrobe, smoothing her wild hair with the uncuffed hand. "I had to pee *so bad,*" she said, sounding almost hysterical with relief.

She walked over to the table and picked up something small and silver.

"See," she said to her sister, "he left me the key. Just not where I could reach it."

Mylissa, overcome by absolutely everything, sank down onto the couch. "I think we have some catching up to do," she said.

Jane gave a small nod. "Yeah, I guess we do."

Mylissa patted the cushion next to her. "So sit your crazy self down, sis. *Now.*"

CHAPTER 24

I TOOK MY BOSS a giant bouquet of apology lilies the next day, and I swore on the grave of my cactus that I'd never disappear like that again. I would not get sick, ever; I wouldn't even take vacation.

Jessica Keller's smile was warmer than usual. "Let's not go too far, Jane," she said. "The secret to success? Underpromise and overdeliver." She placed the bright yellow-and-orange flowers in a crystal vase and gave their petals a fluff. "Just don't ever get food poisoning like that again, okay?"

I nodded vigorously. "From now on, I'm just saying no to mussels."

It wasn't as if I could tell her the truth, after all. Confessing to Mylissa had been hard enough.

I've learned my lesson, I thought as I walked down the hall to my office. Last night I'd ripped up my Rules, and I'd rededicated myself to Netflix.

It was probably impossible to spend fourteen hours chained to a radiator and feel any different about things.

When I got to my desk, my message light was blinking and I had approximately five thousand new emails. The one that caught my eye, though, was from Michael Bishop. The subject line was "New Pitch."

I was proud of my reaction, which was no reaction at all: my heart didn't skip a beat, and my breath didn't quicken. I opened it, hoping only for news that he'd gotten Ned St. John, a media-shy film director, to agree to a *Metropolitan* profile. Pre–Four Seasons, we'd slated it for the October issue.

Dear Jane, the email read. *I hope this note finds you well.* He was keeping it formal—how very professional of him.

I enjoyed our working lunch last month, and I hope you won't consider me rude when I tell you that you are wrong about Ned St. John, whose most recent movie is good but whose personality is execrable. Do not send trees to their deaths over such a cretinous ass.

Instead I propose to feature Kelly Todd, a young female director whose artful "Song of Sorrow" left Cannes audiences blubbering in their seats.

I would also like to say that you are wrong about not seeing me again.

Lunch? Next Friday?

Yours,
Michael B

I scooted my chair back and sighed. Obviously my resolve would be tested. But I would stand firm.

My fingers inched toward the keyboard.

At that moment, Bri scooted into my office with two donuts nestled in a paper napkin. "I missed you yesterday! Look what I got at the ad sales meeting," she said gleefully.

"You're the best," I said, and meant it. I broke off a bit of the chocolate glazed and popped it into my mouth.

"What are you doing tonight?" she asked, helping herself to the coconut cruller. "Want to hit happy hour at Coquine?"

I glanced at my in-box, my messages, and the stack of magazine proofs and groaned for effect. "I have to work, honey."

"Again." Bri sighed. Then she leaned forward and pointed to my wrist. "Hey, *ce qui s'est passé?* What happened? It's all red."

I looked down and saw that she was right. How could I have failed to notice the marks from the handcuffs? I quickly covered them with my sleeve. "Oh, that! My bracelet clasp was stuck, and I was trying to get it off. I'm such a klutz."

Happily, Bri seemed to believe me. "Dumdum," she said affectionately.

You don't know the half of it, I thought.

And at that moment, I made a new rule: *Don't live a life you don't want to talk about.*

Later, I emailed Michael and gave him the go-ahead on the new profile; we could have lunch, I wrote, in the *Metropolitan*

conference room. I'd order in sandwiches from Pain Quoti-
dien.

When I finally left the office at 9 p.m., Eddie the janitor
was emptying the recycling into his giant blue bin.

"Get home safe, Jane," he called.

"Thanks, Eddie. You too."

He chuckled. "Only six more hours and I can call it a night."

I flagged a cab, but as I rode uptown I realized I wasn't
quite ready to call it a night myself. So I had the driver drop
me at a new wine bar just off Amsterdam Avenue.

A test.

With its pressed-tin ceiling and exposed brick lit by strings
of tiny white lights, Hop & Vine felt intimate and welcoming.
I took a seat at the bar and ordered a Pinot, which came in
a fishbowl goblet, accompanied by sliced baguette and butter
flaked with sea salt.

"Anyone joining you?" the bartender asked as he polished
the bar's copper surface. He flashed a sudden grin and leaned
toward me. "Or do you need a little company?"

I glanced around the room. I saw a handful of prospects,
the way I so often had: two banker types, just released from
work and happily guzzling bottles of red, and an attractive,
studious-looking guy—glasses, professorial sport jacket—
thumbing through *The New Yorker*.

But I didn't want to talk to any of them.

I turned back and smiled at the bartender. "It's just me
tonight," I said.

His eyes sparked with interest. "Really," he said, topping off my wine, though I'd barely had a single sip. "A beautiful girl like you?"

I nodded. "But if you don't mind," I added, as gently as I could, "I'd like to just sit here quietly. I brought a good book."

CHAPTER 25

WALKING INTO MY THERAPIST'S office the following Monday morning felt as nerve-racking as going to the Red Room. I wore my primmest dress (black knee-length linen, with a white lace collar), as if it could balance out the hedonistic story I was about to tell.

Because it was time to come clean. Time to reveal my secret, sex-filled summer.

Dr. Jensen smiled as I sank into the familiar leather couch. "Good morning, Jane," he said. "Did you know that today is a special day?"

I nearly spit out my coffee. Had he read my mind? Did he somehow *know* what I was about to do? "Well, uh, yes, maybe?" I stammered, grabbing the nearest pillow and hugging it to my chest like a shield.

"You've been coming here for two full years," he said. "As of today."

I let out the breath I'd been holding in one long whoosh. "Oh!" I said, relieved. "Wow. Well, happy anniversary to us." I mimed lifting a glass for a toast.

"A lot's happened in two years," he said.

"You can say that again."

How far I'd come in those 730 days! First I'd been the worried wife, and then the depressed divorcée, and then what? The naughty nympho? The term made me snicker, and Dr. Jensen seemed to prick up his ears.

"What are you thinking?" he asked.

"I wonder how many times you've asked me that in two years," I said, dodging the question.

He gave a little half-shrug. "It's a big part of the job description."

I took another deep breath and let it out slowly. If I had something to say, there was no time like the present. "I have a confession to make."

Dr. Jensen leaned back in his chair. "All right, then," he said. "I'm listening."

Quickly, before I could lose my courage, I said, "I've been having sex. Lots and lots of it. With strangers."

"You *have?*"

Dr. Jensen had always seemed so unflappable—well, suddenly he looked *seriously flapped.*

Apparently, asking him about other women's sex lives was one thing; admitting to my own wild sex life was another thing entirely.

He put his glasses on and peered at me through them, quickly composing himself. "This seems like something we should talk about, Jane," he said. "It sounds…risky."

I nodded—yes, it had definitely been risky.

And then, in a rush of relief, everything came tumbling out: my first fling with Michael and my cab ride with Ethan; man-shopping at Eataly and cradle-robbing on the High Line; the Red Room and the radiator.

Dr. Jensen's eyes widened several times, but he did his best not to react.

"I'm sure you're judging me," I said, "even though you'll deny it. And that's okay. I'm not ashamed of anything. But I could have been a little…smarter. Safer."

Dr. Jensen shook his head. "My job isn't to make judgments," he said. "My job is to listen, and to draw you out. And, occasionally, to challenge you." He crossed his arms over his chest. "So tell me, Jane. What have you learned from these…experiences?"

"Besides check a guy's pockets for handcuffs?" I asked ruefully.

Dr. Jensen allowed himself a laugh. "Yes," he said. "Besides that."

I had to ponder the question for a minute. It wasn't as if I'd embarked on my great sexual adventure because I was hoping it'd be *educational*.

But, come to think of it, I had learned a lot: about desire, about power, and about human connection—emotional *and* physical. By taking control of my sexuality, I felt like I'd finally taken control of my life.

Dr. Jensen might be doubtful about my methods, but he couldn't argue with the results.

"You know how, at the end of Westerns, the cowboy and his girl always ride off into the sunset?" I asked.

Dr. Jensen frowned slightly. "Jane—"

"This isn't a digression, I swear. And sorry for interrupting you. What I'm trying to say is that I'm happy to spend an hour or two with a handsome cowboy. But when the sun starts to go down, he and his horse can hit the high, dry, and dusty on their own."

"Metaphorically speaking," Dr. Jensen said, trying to follow me.

"Yes. Metaphorically speaking, I'm not riding on the back of anyone's horse *ever again*."

Dr. Jensen laughed. "You certainly have a way with words, Jane."

"Thank you," I said. "The point is, I like being in control. This summer has been about what I want and what I need— not what someone else wants and what someone else needs. And I can't tell you how freeing that is."

"I'm happy for you," Dr. Jensen said. "You're not chained to the past anymore—to James and his betrayal."

"Or handcuffed, as the case may be," I said.

My therapist laughed again. "Exactly. By the way, I brought you something," he said. "For the two years."

He pushed a small cardboard box toward me across the desk.

I leaned forward and looked inside. Nestled in blue tissue paper was a tiny, spiny cactus. A pink flower sat on top of it, just like a little hat.

Delighted, I leapt up and gave Dr. Jensen a hug.

I couldn't help myself. And anyway, it wasn't like I tried to kiss him.

Okay, I thought about it.

But only for a second.

CHAPTER 26

"WHATCHA GOT IN THE box?" the doorman asked as he pushed the heavy glass door open for me.

The question startled me, and I looked up to see a tall, broad-shouldered young man, his navy-and-gold cap tilted rakishly on his head. I hadn't seen this doorman on my way in—or, for that matter, ever before in my life.

"Wait—where's Manny?" I asked. "He was just here."

The new guy grinned, and two deep dimples appeared in his cheeks. "Manny the Silent? He had a plane to catch. Summer vacation—you know how it goes." His voice held the faintest trace of a Brooklyn accent.

"Wow, I never realized until *right this second* that I've never heard Manny speak!" I laughed. "He just nods and smiles."

"Wait until he's off the clock," the new doorman said, leaning toward me confidentially. "Then you'd better staple his lips together if you want him to shut up."

I looked at his shiny brass name tag and then peered up into his dark brown eyes. "I take it you know him, Anthony?"

Anthony nodded. "He's my dad's best friend. I'm filling in for him for the next two weeks." He put his hands on his hips, mock-tough, as he stood in the open doorway. "So are you going to tell me what's in the box or what?"

There was something so charming about his overgrown boyishness that I couldn't help but smile. "Have a look," I said. I held out my prickly new roommate. "It's a cactus of the *Matucana* genus, and I am absolutely not going to kill it."

He laughed. "Are you in the habit of killing succulents?"

"Not on purpose," I said.

"May I?" He took the box from me and gently touched the bloom with the very tip of his finger. "I recommend a good houseplant fertilizer with trace elements. Just dilute it to a quarter strength. Give her plenty of water now, but taper off in the fall."

I raised an eyebrow at him. "Are you a cactus specialist?"

He ducked his head modestly. "No. But I'm getting my PhD in botany."

"Wow. That's really impressive," I said.

"Manny calls me Flower Boy," he said, flushing a little.

"Well, you're a lot bigger than he is," I said. "So next time, you just go like this." I held up a fist and shook it threateningly.

Anthony laughed. "That's a terrible idea," he said.

"You're a lover, not a fighter," I said. "Right?"

"Exactly," Anthony agreed. He smiled at me. "What about you?"

I tossed my hair over my shoulder and smiled in return. "Both," I said.

As I reached out and took my cactus back, my fingers brushed lightly against his. I felt the familiar sweet jolt of electrical attraction.

"Have a good day," I added.

Then I stepped through the door and into the golden morning sunlight.

"Tell me your name at least," Anthony called after me.

I walked a few feet more and then I stopped.

Might I, someday, want the services of a cactus doctor?

I turned around, hurried back to him, and pressed my card into his hand.

"Thank you," Anthony said, flushing again. "Can I call you? Can I call you right now?" He was already patting his pockets for his phone.

Laughing, I waved good-bye, and then, still giggling, I strode down the street.

New York looked spectacular this morning. The yellow cabs, the mirrored office buildings, the emerald-leafed street trees: everything was bright and loud and full of life. I was Jane Avery: single, thirty-five, and living in the best city on earth.

Maybe my phone would start ringing soon, and maybe it wouldn't.

Maybe I'd pick up.

And maybe I'd just keep on walking.

EPILOGUE

"ARE YOU SURE—like, really, *really* sure—you don't want to meet us at Pravda later?" Bri asked as we stepped out of the *Metropolitan* offices into the sweltering August evening. "Come on, Jane, it's Friday! You *need* a vodka gimlet."

I smiled and shook my head. "But you and loverboy *don't* need a third wheel."

"*S'il vous plaît?* You'll be a major conversational aid," Bri pleaded. "Will's amazing, but I really don't need to hear about his triathlon training again. And also..." She stopped.

"Go on," I said—even though I was pretty sure I knew where she was going.

Bri ducked her head and looked slightly embarrassed. "I told Will to bring a friend." Her eyes met mine. "For, um, you."

"I knew it!" I said. "How many times have we talked about my lack of interest in dating?"

"A million?"

"And this makes a million and one." I leaned in and gave

her a quick hug good-bye. "Have a good time tonight. Ask Will about his fartleks."

Bri's eyes grew wide. "His *what?*"

I giggled. "It's a Swedish running term, and I guarantee he knows what it means," I said. "Old fact-checkers never die…"

She grinned. "They just watch TV at home alone on Friday nights, right?"

I didn't answer—I just waved and headed uptown. For one thing, it was a rhetorical question. And for another, I wasn't actually going home.

The truth was, I had a date.

Because I didn't want to be early, I dawdled on my way north. I window-shopped, ducked into a bodega for a Perrier, and stopped to watch a street musician at Columbus and 70th. And then somehow, by the time I looked at my watch again, I was *late*.

I half-jogged fifteen blocks and arrived at the restaurant flustered and sweaty. Pausing outside to catch my breath and smooth my now-frizzy hair, I spied my date through the window.

Anthony, wearing a dark button-down shirt open at the collar, was sitting in a cozy little booth—waiting for me. A server came over and placed a tall glass of beer in front of him, and I watched as Anthony looked up and smiled a bright, boyish smile of gratitude.

There was something so sweet in that look. Something so…*open*—like he was ready to love just about anyone.

And right then, I realized my mistake. Dating someone so young and enthusiastic and affectionate would be like dating a *puppy*. Albeit a puppy who could nurse my cactus back to life, should the prickly little thing ever require it. (But hey, so far it was doing *just fine*.)

And that's how I found myself turning on my heel and hurrying away, leaving Anthony to drink his frothy craft beer—as Bri would say—*tout seul*. All alone.

I wasn't proud of myself, not for one second. But I knew that what I was doing was right.

I was almost back to my apartment when it occurred to me that I was starving, and that my refrigerator contained only apples, pita bread, and a takeout container of Al's hummus: nothing that would make even a halfway acceptable dinner. So I ducked into a little Italian place on the corner of Columbus and 98th. Immediately I was met by the comforting smell of a garlicky, tomatoey ragù.

Most of the tables were occupied, so I took a seat at the narrow marble bar. The bartender—black-haired, potbellied, with a name tag that said FRANCO—greeted me graciously.

"I have a beautiful Amarone on special tonight," he said, his voice a deep baritone. "Would you like a glass?"

"I'd love one," I said. I scanned the menu quickly. "And can I have the agnolotti with the taleggio and wild mushrooms?"

He gave a small smile and an even smaller bow. "Of course, miss," he said. "Excellent choice."

When the pasta came, I devoured every cheesy, mushroomy molecule of it. And then, sated, I leaned back, took a sip of my wine, and looked around the room. I noticed the lovely orchid display at the hostess stand, the pretty, faded prints on the wall, and the tiny crystal chandeliers dangling from the ceiling, illuminating everything with a warm golden glow.

How many times had I walked past this place? And I'd never noticed it before, though it had obviously been here for years.

New York City: it slowly kept revealing itself, unfolding like one of those old-fashioned accordion postcards. A person could never see half of its secrets.

When I turned back to my wine, I noticed that the seat next to mine was now occupied. By—you guessed it—a man.

He was a few years older than me. His dark hair was cut very short, and his eyes, behind a pair of excellent vintage glasses, were almost black. He was drinking a scotch, neat.

Was it my imagination, or did the room suddenly get warmer? I took a quick sip of ice water and pretended I hadn't seen him.

But he had obviously seen me.

Out of the corner of my eye, I watched him lean, ever so slightly, toward me. "Hi," he said quietly. "I like your dress."

I inhaled. Exhaled.

Then I slowly uncrossed my legs under the smooth black chiffon of the Dress, and I turned toward him. "Oh, this old thing?" I said, smiling.

Prepare for a courtroom shocker you'll never see coming

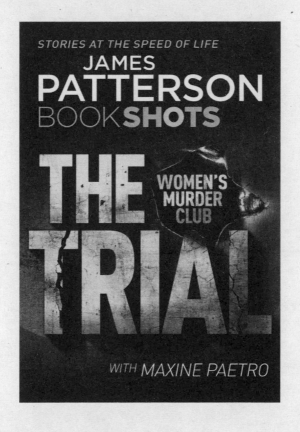

STORIES AT THE SPEED OF LIFE

JAMES
PATTERSON
BOOK**SHOTS**

THE

WOMEN'S
MURDER
CLUB

TRIAL

WITH MAXINE PAETRO

Read on for an extract

IT WAS THAT CRAZY period between Thanksgiving and Christmas when work overflowed, time raced, and there wasn't enough light between dawn and dusk to get everything done.

Still, our gang of four, what we call the Women's Murder Club, always had a spouse-free holiday get-together dinner of drinks and bar food.

Yuki Castellano had picked the place.

It was called Uncle Maxie's Top Hat and was a bar and grill that had been a fixture in the Financial District for 150 years. It was decked out with art deco prints and mirrors on the walls, and a large, neon-lit clock behind the bar dominated the room. Maxie's catered to men in smart suits and women in tight skirts and spike heels who wore good jewelry.

I liked the place and felt at home there in a Mickey Spillane kind of way. Case in point: I was wearing straight-legged pants, a blue gabardine blazer, a Glock in my shoulder holster, and flat lace-up shoes. I stood in the bar area, slowly turning my head as I looked around for my BFFs.

"Lindsay. Yo."

Cindy Thomas waved her hand from the table tucked under the spiral staircase. I waved back, moved toward the nook inside the cranny. Claire Washburn was wearing a trench coat over her scrubs, with a button on the lapel that read SUPPORT OUR TROOPS. She peeled off her coat and gave me a hug and a half.

Cindy was also in her work clothes: cords and a bulky sweater, with a peacoat slung over the back of her chair. If I'd ducked under the table, I'm sure I would have seen steel-toed boots. Cindy was a crime reporter of note, and she was wearing her on-the-job hound dog clothes.

She blew me a couple of kisses, and Yuki stood up to give me her seat and a jasmine-scented smack on the cheek. She had clearly come from court, where she worked as a pro bono defense attorney for the poor and hopeless. Still, she was dressed impeccably, in pinstripes and pearls.

I took the chair across from Claire. She sat between Cindy and Yuki with her back to the room, and we all scooched up to the smallish glass-and-chrome table.

If it hasn't been said, we four are a mutual heart, soul, and work society in which we share our cases and views of the legal system, as well as our personal lives. Right now the girls were worried about me.

Three of us were married—me, Claire, and Yuki—and Cindy had a standing offer of a ring and vows to be exchanged in Grace Cathedral. Until very recently you couldn't have found four more happily hooked-up women. Then the bottom fell out of my marriage to Joe Molinari, the father of my child and a man I shared everything with, including my secrets.

We had had it so good, we kissed and made up before our fights were over. It was the typical: "You are right." "No, you are!"

Then Joe went missing during possibly the worst weeks of my life.

I'm a homicide cop, and I know when someone is telling me the truth and when things do not add up.

Joe missing in action had not added up. Because of that I had worried almost to panic. Where was he? Why hadn't he checked in? Why were my calls bouncing off his full mailbox? Was he still alive?

As the crisscrossed threads of espionage, destruction, and mass murder were untangled, Joe finally made his curtain call with stories of his past and present lives that I'd never heard before. I found plenty of reason not to trust him anymore.

Even he would agree. I think anyone would.

It's not news that once trust is broken, it's damned hard to superglue it back together. And for me it might take more time and belief in Joe's confession than I actually had.

I still loved him. We'd shared a meal when he came to see our baby, Julie. We didn't make any moves toward getting divorced that night, but we didn't make love, either. Our relationship was now like the Cold War in the eighties between Russia and the USA, a strained but practical peace called détente.

Now, as I sat with my friends, I tried to put Joe out of my

mind, secure in the knowledge that my nanny was looking after Julie and that the home front was safe. I ordered a favorite holiday drink, a hot buttered rum, and a rare steak sandwich with Uncle Maxie's hot chili sauce.

My girlfriends were deep in criminal cross talk about Claire's holiday overload of corpses, Cindy's new cold case she'd exhumed from the *San Francisco Chronicle*'s dead letter files, and Yuki's hoped-for favorable verdict for her client, an underage drug dealer. I was almost caught up when Yuki said, "Linds, I gotta ask. Any Christmas plans with Joe?"

And that's when I was saved by the bell. My phone rang.

My friends said in unison, "NO PHONES."

It was the rule, but I'd forgotten—again.

I reached into my bag for my phone, saying, "Look, I'm turning it off."

But I saw that the call was from Rich Conklin, my partner and Cindy's fiancé. She recognized his ring tone on my phone.

"There goes our party," she said, tossing her napkin into the air.

"Linds?" said Conklin.

"Rich, can this wait? I'm in the middle—"

"It's Kingfisher. He's in a shoot-out with cops at the Vault. There've been casualties."

"But—Kingfisher is *dead*."

"Apparently, he's been resurrected."

MY PARTNER WAS DOUBLE-PARKED and waiting for me outside Uncle Maxie's, with the engine running and the flashers on. I got into the passenger seat of the unmarked car, and Richie handed me my vest. He's that way, like a younger version of a big brother. He thinks of me, watches out for me, and I try to do the same for him.

He watched me buckle up, then he hit the siren and stepped on the gas.

We were about five minutes from the Vault, a class A nightclub on the second floor of a former Bank of America building.

"Fill me in," I said to my partner.

"Call came in to 911 about ten minutes ago," Conklin said as we tore up California Street. "A kitchen worker said he recognized Kingfisher out in the bar. He was still trying to convince 911 that it was an emergency when shots were fired inside the club."

"Watch out on our right."

Richie yanked the wheel hard left to avoid an indecisive panel truck, then jerked it hard right and took a turn onto Sansome.

"You okay?" he asked.

I had been known to get carsick in jerky high-speed chases when I wasn't behind the wheel.

"I'm fine. Keep talking."

My partner told me that a second witness reported to first officers that three men were talking to two women at the bar. One of the men yelled, "No one screws with the King." Shots were fired. The women were killed.

"Caller didn't leave his name."

I was gripping both the dash and the door, and had both feet on imaginary brakes, but my mind was occupied with King-fisher. He was a Mexican drug cartel boss, a psycho with a history of brutality and revenge, and a penchant for settling his scores personally.

Richie was saying, "Patrol units arrived as the shooters were attempting to flee through the front entrance. Someone saw the tattoo on the back of the hand of one of the shooters. I talked to Brady," Conklin said, referring to our lieutenant. "If that shooter is Kingfisher and survives, he's ours."

I WANTED THE KING on death row for the normal reasons. He was to the drug and murder trade as al-Baghdadi was to terrorism. But I also had personal reasons.

Earlier that year a cadre of dirty San Francisco cops from our division had taken down a number of drug houses for their own financial gain. One drug house in particular yielded a payoff of five to seven million in cash and drugs. Whether those cops knew it beforehand or not, the stolen loot belonged to Kingfisher—and he wanted it back.

The King took his revenge but was still short a big pile of dope and dollars.

So he turned his sights on me.

I was the primary homicide inspector on the dirty-cop case.

Using his own twisted logic, the King demanded that I personally recover and return his property. Or else.

It was a threat and a promise, and of course I couldn't deliver.

From that moment on I had protection all day and night, every day and night, but protection isn't enough when your tormentor is like a ghost. We had grainy photos and shoddy footage from cheap surveillance cameras on file. We had a blurry picture of a tattoo on the back of his left hand.

That was all.

After his threat I couldn't cross the street from my apartment to my car without fear that Kingfisher would drop me dead in the street.

A week after the first of many threatening phone calls, the calls stopped. A report came in from the Mexican federal police saying that they had turned up the King's body in a shallow grave in Baja. That's what they said.

I had wondered then if the King was really dead. If the freaking nightmare was truly over.

I had just about convinced myself that my family and I were safe. Now the breaking news confirmed that my gut reaction had been right. Either the Mexican police had lied, or the King had tricked them with a dead doppelganger buried in the sand.

A few minutes ago the King had been identified by a kitchen worker at the Vault. If true, why had he surfaced again in San Francisco? Why had he chosen to show his face in a nightclub filled with people? Why shoot two women inside that club? And my number one question: Could we bring him in alive and take him to trial?

Please, God. Please.

OUR CAR RADIO WAS barking, crackling, and squealing at a high pitch as cars were directed to the Vault, in the middle of the block on Walnut Street. Cruisers and ambulances screamed past us as Conklin and I closed in on the scene. I badged the cop at the perimeter, and immediately after, Rich backed our car into a gap in the pack of law enforcement vehicles, parking it across the street from the Vault.

The Vault was built of stone block. It had two centered large glass doors, now shattered, with a half-circular window across the doorframe. Flanking the doors were two tall windows, capped with demilune windows, glass also shot out.

Shooters inside the Vault were using the granite doorframe as a barricade as they leaned out and fired on the uniformed officers positioned behind their car doors.

Conklin and I got out of our car with our guns drawn and crouched beside our wheel wells. Adrenaline whipped my heart into a gallop. I watched everything with clear eyes, and yet my mind flooded with memories of past shoot-outs. I had been shot and almost died. All three of my partners had been shot, one of them fatally.

And now I had a baby at home.

A cop at the car to my left shouted, *"Christ!"*

Her gun spun out of her hand and she grabbed her shoulder as she dropped to the asphalt. Her partner ran to her, dragged her toward the rear of the car, and called in, "Officer down." Just then SWAT arrived in force with a small caravan of SUVs and a ballistic armored transport vehicle as big as a bus. The SWAT commander used his megaphone, calling to the shooters, who had slipped back behind the fortresslike walls of the Vault.

"All exits are blocked. There's nowhere to run, nowhere to hide. Toss out the guns, now."

The answer to the SWAT commander was a fusillade of gunfire that pinged against steel chassis. SWAT hit back with automatic weapons, and two men fell out of the doorway onto the pavement.

The shooting stopped, leaving an echoing silence.

The commander used his megaphone and called out, "You. Put your gun down and we won't shoot. Fair warning. We're coming in."

"WAIT. I give up," said an accented voice. "Hands up, see?"

"Come all the way out. Come to me," said the SWAT commander.

I could see him from where I stood.

The last of the shooters was a short man with a café au

lait complexion, a prominent nose, dark hair that was brushed back. He was wearing a well-cut suit with a blood-splattered white shirt as he came out through the doorway with his hands up.

Two guys in tactical gear grabbed him and slammed him over the hood of an SUV, then cuffed and arrested him.

The SWAT commander dismounted from the armored vehicle. I recognized him as Reg Covington. We'd worked together before. Conklin and I walked over to where Reg was standing beside the last of the shooters.

Covington said, "Boxer. Conklin. You know this guy?"

He stood the shooter up so I could get a good look at his face. I'd never met Kingfisher. I compared the real-life suspect with my memory of the fuzzy videos I'd seen of Jorge Sierra, a.k.a. the King.

"Let me see his hands," I said.

It was a miracle that my voice sounded steady, even to my own ears. I was sweating and my breathing was shallow. My gut told me that this was the man.

Covington twisted the prisoner's hands so that I could see the backs of them. On the suspect's left hand was the tattoo of a kingfisher, the same as the one in the photo in Kingfisher's slim file.

I said to our prisoner, "Mr. Sierra. I'm Sergeant Boxer. Do you need medical attention?"

"Mouth-to-mouth resuscitation, maybe."

Covington jerked him to his feet and said, "We'll take good care of him. Don't worry."

He marched the King to the waiting police wagon, and I watched as he was shackled and chained to the bar before the door was closed.

Covington slapped the side of the van, and it took off as CSI and the medical examiner's van moved in and SWAT thundered into the Vault to clear the scene.

CONKLIN AND I JOINED the patrol cops who were talking to the Vault's freaked-out customers, now milling nervously in the taped-off section of the street.

We wanted an eyewitness description of the shooter or shooters in the *act* of killing two women in the bar.

That's not what we got.

One by one and in pairs, they answered our questions about what they had seen. It all came down to statements like *I was under the table. I was in the bathroom. I wasn't wearing my glasses. I couldn't see the bar. I didn't look up until I heard screaming, and then I ran to the back.*

We noted the sparse statements, took names and contact info, and asked each person to call if something occurred to him or her later. I was handing out my card when a patrolman came over, saying, "Sergeant, this is Ryan Kelly. He tends bar here. Mr. Kelly says he watched a conversation escalate into the shooting."

Thank God.

Ryan Kelly was about twenty-five, with dark, spiky hair. His skin was pale with shock.

Conklin said, "Mr. Kelly, what can you tell us?"

Kelly didn't hesitate.

"Two women were at the bar, both knockouts, and they were into each other. Touching knees, hands, the like. The blonde was in her twenties, tight black dress, drinking wine coolers. The other was brunette, in her thirties but in great shape, drinking a Scotch on the rocks, in a white dress, or maybe it was beige.

"Three guys, looked Mexican, came over. They were dressed right, between forty and fifty, I'd say. The brunette saw their reflections in the backbar mirror and she jumped. Like, *Oh, my God.* Then she introduced the blonde as 'my friend Cameron.'"

The bartender was on a roll and needed no encouragement to keep talking. He said there had been some back-and-forth among the five people, that the brunette had been nervous but the short man with the combed-back hair had been super calm and played with her.

"Like he was glad to meet her friend," said Kelly. "He asked me to mix him a drink called a Pastinaca. Has five ingredients that have to be poured in layers, and I had no open elderflower. There was a new bottle under the bar. So I ducked down to find it among a shitload of other bottles.

"Then I heard someone say in a really strong voice, 'No one screws with the King.' Something like that. There's a shot, and another right after it. Loud *pop, pop.* And then a bunch more. I had, like, a heart attack and flattened out on the floor behind the bar. There was screaming like crazy. I stayed down until our manager found me and said, 'Come on. Get outta here.'"

I asked, "You didn't see who did the shooting?"

Kelly said, "No. Okay for me to go now? I've told this to about three of you. My wife is going nuts waiting for me at home."

We took Kelly's contact information, and when Covington signaled us that the Vault was clear, Conklin and I gloved up, stepped around the dead men, their spilled blood, guns, and spent shells in the doorway, and went inside.

I KNEW THE VAULT'S layout: the ground floor of the former bank had been converted into a high-end haberdashery. Access to the nightclub upstairs was by the elevators at the rear of the store.

Conklin and I took in the scene. Bloody shoe prints tracked across the marble floors. Toppled clothing racks and mannequins lay across the aisles, but nothing moved.

We crossed the floor with care and took an elevator to the second-floor club, the scene of the shooting and a forensics investigation disaster.

Tables and chairs had been overturned in the customers' rush toward the fire exit. There were no surveillance cameras, and the floor was tacky with spilled booze and blood.

We picked our way around abandoned personal property and over to the long, polished bar, where two women in expensive clothing lay dead. One, blond, had collapsed across the bar top, and the other, dark-haired, had fallen dead at her feet.

The lighting was soft and unfocused, but still, I could see that the blond woman had been shot between the eyes and had taken slugs in her chest and arms. The woman on the floor had a bullet hole through the draped white silk across her chest, and there was another in her neck.

"Both shot at close range," Richie said.

He plucked a beaded bag off the floor and opened it, and I did the same with the second bag, a metallic leather clutch.

According to their driver's licenses, the brunette was Lucille Alison Stone and the blonde was Cameron Whittaker. I took pictures, and then Conklin and I carefully cat-walked out of the bar the way we had come.

As we were leaving, we passed Charlie Clapper, our CSI director, coming in with his crew.

Clapper was a former homicide cop and always looked like he'd stepped out of a Grecian Formula commercial. Neat. Composed. With comb marks in his hair. Always thorough, never a grandstander, he was one of the SFPD's MVPs.

"What's your take?" he asked us.

"It was overkill," I said. "Two women were shot to death at point-blank range and then shot some more. Three men were reportedly seen talking to them before the shooting. Two of them are in your capable hands until Claire takes them. We have one alive, being booked now."

"The news is out. You think he's Kingfisher."

"Could be. I hope so. I really hope this is our lucky day."

JAMES
PATTERSON
BOOK**SHOTS**
OUT THIS MONTH

THE TRIAL: A WOMEN'S MURDER CLUB THRILLER

An accused killer will do anything to disrupt his own trial, including a courtroom shocker that Lindsay Boxer will never see coming.

AIRPORT: CODE RED

A major terrorist cell sets a devastating plan in motion. Their target? One of the world's busiest airports.

LITTLE BLACK DRESS

Can a little black dress change everything? What begins as one woman's fantasy is about to go too far.

LEARNING TO RIDE

City girl Madeline Harper never wanted to love a cowboy. But rodeo king Tanner Callen might change her mind ... and win her heart.

JAMES PATTERSON

BOOK**SHOTS**

COMING SOON

CHASE: A MICHAEL BENNETT THRILLER

A man falls to his death in an apparent accident. But why does
he have the fingerprints of another man who is already dead?
Detective Michael Bennett is on the case.

LET'S PLAY MAKE-BELIEVE

Christy and Marty just met, and it's love at first sight. Or is it?
One of them is playing a dangerous game – and only one will survive.

DEAD HEAT

Detective Carvalho is investigating the disappearance of an
Australian athlete on the day of the opening ceremony of the 2016
Olympic Games. The case is about to take a deadly turn...

THE McCULLAGH INN IN MAINE

Chelsea O'Kane escapes to Maine to build a new life – until
she runs into Jeremy Holland, an old flame...

ALSO BY JAMES PATTERSON

ALEX CROSS NOVELS

Along Came a Spider

Kiss the Girls

Jack and Jill

Cat and Mouse

Pop Goes the Weasel

Roses are Red

Violets are Blue

Four Blind Mice

The Big Bad Wolf

London Bridges

Mary, Mary

Cross

Double Cross

Cross Country

Alex Cross's Trial (*with Richard DiLallo*)

I, Alex Cross

Cross Fire

Kill Alex Cross

Merry Christmas, Alex Cross

Alex Cross, Run

Cross My Heart

Hope to Die

Cross Justice

THE WOMEN'S MURDER CLUB SERIES

1st to Die

2nd Chance (*with Andrew Gross*)

3rd Degree (*with Andrew Gross*)

4th of July (*with Maxine Paetro*)

The 5th Horseman (*with Maxine Paetro*)

The 6th Target (*with Maxine Paetro*)

7th Heaven (*with Maxine Paetro*)

8th Confession (*with Maxine Paetro*)

9th Judgement (*with Maxine Paetro*)

10th Anniversary (*with Maxine Paetro*)

11th Hour (*with Maxine Paetro*)

12th of Never (*with Maxine Paetro*)

Unlucky 13 (*with Maxine Paetro*)

14th Deadly Sin (*with Maxine Paetro*)

15th Affair (*with Maxine Paetro*)

DETECTIVE MICHAEL BENNETT SERIES

Step on a Crack (*with Michael Ledwidge*)

Run for Your Life (*with Michael Ledwidge*)

Worst Case (*with Michael Ledwidge*)

Tick Tock (*with Michael Ledwidge*)

I, Michael Bennett (*with Michael Ledwidge*)

Gone (*with Michael Ledwidge*)

Burn (*with Michael Ledwidge*)

Alert (*with Michael Ledwidge*)

PRIVATE NOVELS

Private (*with Maxine Paetro*)

Private London (*with Mark Pearson*)

Private Games (*with Mark Sullivan*)

Private: No. 1 Suspect (*with Maxine Paetro*)

Private Berlin (*with Mark Sullivan*)
Private Down Under (*with Michael White*)
Private L.A. (*with Mark Sullivan*)
Private India (*with Ashwin Sanghi*)
Private Vegas (*with Maxine Paetro*)
Private Sydney (*with Kathryn Fox*)
Private Paris (*with Mark Sullivan*)
The Games (*with Mark Sullivan*)

NYPD RED SERIES

NYPD Red (*with Marshall Karp*)
NYPD Red 2 (*with Marshall Karp*)
NYPD Red 3 (*with Marshall Karp*)
NYPD Red 4 (*with Marshall Karp*)

STAND-ALONE THRILLERS

Sail (*with Howard Roughan*)
Swimsuit (*with Maxine Paetro*)
Don't Blink (*with Howard Roughan*)
Postcard Killers (*with Liza Marklund*)
Toys (*with Neil McMahon*)
Now You See Her (*with Michael Ledwidge*)
Kill Me If You Can (*with Marshall Karp*)
Guilty Wives (*with David Ellis*)
Zoo (*with Michael Ledwidge*)
Second Honeymoon (*with Howard Roughan*)
Mistress (*with David Ellis*)

Invisible (*with David Ellis*)
The Thomas Berryman Number
Truth or Die (*with Howard Roughan*)
Murder House (*with David Ellis*)

NON-FICTION

Torn Apart (*with Hal and Cory Friedman*)
The Murder of King Tut (*with Martin Dugard*)

ROMANCE

Sundays at Tiffany's (*with Gabrielle Charbonnet*)
The Christmas Wedding (*with Richard DiLallo*)
First Love (*with Emily Raymond*)

OTHER TITLES

Miracle at Augusta (*with Peter de Jonge*)

BOOKSHOTS

Black & Blue (*with Candice Fox*)
Break Point (*with Lee Stone*)
Cross Kill
Private Royals (*with Rees Jones*)
The Hostage (*with Robert Gold*)
Zoo 2 (*with Max DiLallo*)
Heist (*with Rees Jones*)
Hunted (*with Andrew Holmes*)